PUFFIN BOOKS

Dandelion Clocks

Rebecca Westcott was born in Chester. She went to Exeter University to train as a teacher and has had a variety of teaching jobs that have taken her to some very interesting places, including a Category C male prison. She started writing a diary when she was eight years old, although she had no idea that one day her entries would be used to help her write a novel. Rebecca currently teaches in a primary school and lives in Dorset with her husband and three children. *Dandelion Clocks* is her first book.

Dandelion Clocks

REBECCA WESTCOTT

PUFFIN

PUFFIN BOOKS

Published by the Penguin Group
Penguin Books Ltd, 80 Strand, London WC2R ORL, England
Penguin Group (USA) Inc., 375 Hudson Street, New York, New York 10014, USA
Penguin Group (Canada), 90 Eglinton Avenue East, Suite 700, Toronto, Ontario, Canada M4P 2Y3
(a division of Pearson Penguin Canada Inc.)
Penguin Ireland, 25 St Stephen's Green, Dublin 2, Ireland (a division of Penguin Books Ltd)
Penguin Group (Australia), 707 Collins Street, Melbourne, Victoria 3008, Australia
(a division of Pearson Australia Group Pty Ltd)
Penguin Books India Pvt Ltd, 11 Community Centre, Panchsheel Park, New Delhi – 110 017, India
Penguin Group (NZ), 67 Apollo Drive, Rosedale, Auckland 0632, New Zealand
(a division of Pearson New Zealand Ltd)
Penguin Books (South Africa) (Pty) Ltd, Block D, Rosebank Office Park,
181 Jan Smuts Avenue, Parktown North, Gauteng 2193, South Africa

Penguin Books Ltd, Registered Offices: 80 Strand, London WC2R ORL, England

puffinbooks.com

First published 2014
001

Set in 12.5/16.5pt Sabon LT Std
Typeset by Jouve (UK), Milton Keynes
Printed in Great Britain by Clays Ltd, St Ives plc

British Library Cataloguing in Publication Data
A CIP catalogue record for this book is available from the British Library

ISBN: 978-0-141-34899-5

www.greenpenguin.co.uk

MIX
Paper from
responsible sources
FSC™ C018179
www.fsc.org

Penguin Books is committed to a sustainable
future for our business, our readers and our planet.
This book is made from Forest Stewardship
Council™ certified paper.

For Zachary, Georgia and Reuben,
who definitely know how to live life loudly.
And for Adam, who fills our lives with
adventures and excitement.

Contents

Three Months After

I sometimes think about the box buried deep at the back of my wardrobe and wonder if I'll ever open it up again. I wonder if her soul is in there, desperate to get out and be free. I wonder what she'd say to me if she could see how I've become – but I don't think about this for too long because I think I know what she'd say and I don't agree with her. To laugh, to enjoy, to live is to forget – and I will never forgive myself if I allow that to happen. And actually, she left me so she doesn't get a chance to have an opinion. If she wanted to have a say in how I live my life then she should have stayed, shouldn't she? She shouldn't have left me alone with a box of old, rubbish diaries that are no use to me at all.

She shouldn't have gone.

Thirteen Weeks Before

If it were possible to actually die of embarrassment, then right now, I would be officially *dead*. There should be some sort of Charter, or human rights Act, that stops every mum from behaving as if she is the first person in the world to become a mother. It's like my mum has no idea that women the world over have been parenting forever and have not felt the need to interfere in every teeny little detail of a child's life. People grow up every day, even without their interfering mothers and their totally unwanted help and 'advice'.

I so nearly got away with it as well. I've been planning for ages and saving my allowance so that I didn't have to ask Mum or Dad for extra – I knew they'd go mental if they thought that I'd gone against their wishes *and* got them to pay for it into the bargain.

I'd done all my research – which wasn't that hard as the only place in this miserable town that you can get your ears pierced is Hair & Things, a totally lame girly shop that sells jewellery and hairbands and lots and lots of pots of nail varnish in neon colours – and Alice called for me this morning as we'd agreed.

When we got to the shop there was a queue. I started to feel a bit nervous and wished I'd brought my camera. Taking photos always clears my mind of everything else and the girl waiting in front of me had this amazing purple and pink hair that would have made a brilliant photograph. Alice told me that it wouldn't hurt any more than the time I was stung by a bee at Sports Day – which wasn't actually reassuring cos that was agony. Anyway, it came to my turn and I sat on the stool in the window.

I've never been sure why they put the stool in the window – but I know now. It's so that when your nosy, bossy mother happens to walk past on her way to the supermarket and sees you sitting there about to 'violate your beautiful body', she can push her way into the shop, yelling at the top of her voice and demanding that the, frankly terrified, shop assistant explain herself 'this very instant, young lady'.

She then went on to ask, in a piercing voice that carried all the way to the back of the shop (where I definitely saw some girls from school lurking and sniggering), how a reputable shop could allow a young girl to disfigure herself. The shop manager had bustled over by this time and started telling Mum that I'd said I was over sixteen, but Mum burst out laughing in a not-very-amused way and asked the manager to take a good look at me and did I *look* like I could possibly be over sixteen? The manager said that no, now that she thought about it, I looked nowhere near sixteen and could she offer Mum a £5 gift voucher to make up for the mistake?

I have no idea what Mum said in response as I was too busy dealing with shrinking into the floor.

By now the girls from school were openly listening to every comment and nudging each other and laughing. Alice, star that she is, stayed by my side but had turned a particularly unflattering shade of pink.

Mum, having made mincemeat of the manager and vowing never to darken the door of Hair & Things again as long as she lived, turned and stormed back out on to the street.

It was obvious that she expected me and Alice

to follow her, which we did. Mum was waiting for us outside and without saying a single word, walked us to the car. The whole way back to Alice's nobody said a thing. Alice and I kept looking at each other – I half wanted to laugh but every time I thought about what had just happened, and how it would have spread round Facebook like wildfire by the time I went to school on Monday morning, I lost my sense of humour. Alice just looked petrified – my mum can be pretty scary when she wants to be.

We dropped Alice off at her house, Mum still not speaking. Alice gave my hand a squeeze and mouthed 'Good luck' at me. We both knew that I was really going to need it.

Mum drove off but then she stopped the car round the corner. I braced myself. The thing about my mum is that she talks. And talks. I reckon the armed forces have missed a trick when it comes to fighting terrorism and defending the free world – they should send Mum in and let her lecture the enemy into surrendering. A couple of hours with her and they'd be begging to be released with eternal promises of good behaviour and a firm understanding of the consequences if they stepped out of line . . .

This time, though, she surprised me. I thought she'd be furious that I'd gone behind her and Dad's back – not that Dad has much of an opinion on the subject. He refuses to talk about it – says as he's not a girl that he doesn't understand what all the fuss is about. So typical – he always backs Mum in any argument. We've had endless conversations about me getting my ears pierced, and she always says I have to wait until I'm thirteen and it'll be a good, appropriate way to mark my teenage years. I always say that it's not a big deal; all my mates have got funkier parents who let them have stuff done and being eleven is virtually the same as being thirteen anyway, so what's the difference?

She didn't even mention the deceit, though. Instead, she started talking to me about the risk that I'd taken and did I understand what could happen if piercings went wrong? Did I actually understand about infections and scarring? I think the words 'ugly disfigurement' were used but I wasn't really listening. I was too busy wondering what she was going to dream up for me as a punishment – sorry, a consequence.

Mum prides herself on making the 'consequence' fit the crime and I was trying to figure out how she could possibly do that this time. By making me pierce my own ears with a needle and an ice cube? By writing a letter to all Hair & Things shops asking them to display my photo in the window and issue me with a lifetime ban? I didn't actually hear her when she said it the first time, so she had to repeat herself (and she hates doing that).

'Olivia – are you actually listening to me? I said, I'll find a decent place that knows what they're doing, and we'll go together and get your ears pierced. If it matters that much to you then fine, but I don't want you sneaking off without telling me.'

Wow. Didn't see that one coming. I'm actually going to have my ears pierced! I will no longer be the only girl in my year with boring, plain ears (I mean, there's probably a *few* other people who haven't got their ears pierced, but I'm not interested in them). Already I'm planning what sort of earrings I'll buy. I reckon I'll look fantastic. I've seen a pair of bright, wooden parrots that I could wear in a jokey, not serious way – that'd be hilarious! And for school I'll get some tiny, silver flowers – maybe daisies. We're meant to wear plain studs but nobody does.

I can't believe my mum is actually agreeing to

this! I love her *so much*! But I'm also still mad at her and Monday morning is going to be a nightmare. Everyone will know about what just happened in town. Maybe I will actually die of humiliation over the weekend – and then she'll be sorry as she sheds endless tears of regret over my cold, sad, unpierced body. She is so utterly annoying and embarrassing. She seriously doesn't have a clue about what it's like to be eleven. And I bet she doesn't get around to taking me to have my ears pierced until I am actually thirteen anyway.

Twelve Weeks Before

Sometimes I wish that I was an only child. No constant compromising and making sure that everything is fair. I think about what life would be like without the responsibilities of looking after my brother and imagine how utterly amazing it would be. Even though my brother, Isaac, is three years older than me, I often feel like I'm the bigger one – just without the big sister title. Some days, he seriously does not have a clue and ends up getting in all sorts of trouble if I'm not there to watch out for him. It's definitely a boy thing – sometimes he just seems to get it all wrong. It's also a bit of an Isaac thing too – he can't help it and I know it's not actually his fault, but when it's a tricky day with Isaac I sometimes can't help wishing that he was more like other people's brothers.

Today was one of those days. Mum asked me to go down to the shop and get her some milk and to take Isaac with me. I really didn't want to but she said that he'd spent enough time in his room playing computer games and he needed the fresh air.

Mum and Dad worry a lot about Isaac. They think he's got no friends and they're always trying to figure out ways to stop him playing on his PlayStation. This makes me laugh – they think they know everything but they have no idea that Isaac has loads of friends. He meets up with them online and the reason he likes playing games in the middle of the night is so he can play with his friends who live on the other side of the world when it's their daytime. If Mum and Dad stop his PlayStation time then he really *won't* have any friends.

I know all about Internet safety because they go on about it loads at school. Isaac doesn't really get stuff like that, so I keep an eye on what he's doing and who he's talking to. He knows that he can never meet his computer friends in real life but that's the thing – he'd never actually want to. Isaac doesn't do well when he has to speak to people but he can be really funny when he's online. Anyway, I think most of his friends are kids just like him.

Mum wasn't going to give up on me dragging Isaac out. She knows that I can get him to do things that nobody else can – which is a pain pretty much all of the time cos I end up being the one who has to go into his smelly room and bargain with him.

I trudge up the stairs.

'Sooner you go, sooner you'll be back!' calls Mum after me. Yeah – that's a helpful comment; thanks a lot, Mum.

I knock on Isaac's door in the right way – he refuses to answer unless you do three knocks followed by two knocks followed by one knock. The day he decided that one, it took us an hour to get it right and persuade him to come downstairs for tea. Mum's macaroni cheese was so congealed that it would only come out of the dish in one large lump. Dad ended up going to KFC and buying us a family meal (which Isaac refused to eat as we usually have takeaway on Friday nights but it was only Wednesday).

'Come on – Mum wants us to get her some milk,' I call through the door.

No reply.

'Isaac, I know you heard me. Open the door or I'll start singing!'

That does the trick. Isaac hates my singing but I try not to take it too personally because he hates all singing. The door opens a crack, but by the time I've pushed through, Isaac is back on his PlayStation chair. Dad said if he was going to spend so many hours playing games each day, they could at least make sure he had good posture, so they bought him a massively expensive special chair.

'Liv to Isaac – move your backside – we're going out into the big wide world!'

Isaac shows no sign of actually having heard me.

'Come on, Isaac – I haven't got all day,' I sigh, suddenly feeling tired.

Nothing. No reaction whatsoever. Have I mentioned that my brother can be very stubborn?

'Get up, Isaac, *now*!' I snap.

'I don't want to go out,' he mutters, firing a rocket into a zombie.

'I don't care if you want to or not – we're going.'

He ignores me so I have to play my ace card.

'You know what day it is, don't you?' I say casually.

'I'm not stupid, Liv – it's Saturday,' Isaac growls. He gets very sensitive if he thinks anyone is calling him thick.

'Not just *any* old Saturday,' I say, and I can see that I finally have his attention. His eyes dart to the wall planner above his desk and then he springs to his feet, PlayStation controller tumbling to the floor.

'Hey – steady on!' I yelp as he shoves past me and barrels down the stairs, just avoiding the cat who has been snoozing in the sunlight on the bottom step. She's used to Isaac, though, and darts out of his way, giving him a very dirty look.

'Wait a minute – we need our coats on,' I yell at him, but he is already out of the front door and heading down the path, oblivious to the rain that has appeared from nowhere. I grab my coat and my old camera (you never know when the perfect photo opportunity might turn up), and Mum, who has raced through from the kitchen, shoves Isaac's jacket and a £5 note at me.

'Thanks, Liv!' she shouts as I sprint after Isaac.

I finally catch up with him before he steps off the pavement. Our street joins on to a busy main road – I didn't think he'd try to cross it; he hasn't tried that before, but you can never be entirely sure what Isaac will do next, and one thing I do know is that he is *not* familiar with the Green Cross Code.

'Wait for me – I'm not an Olympic athlete, you know!' I puff, as I stagger up next to him.

'I do know that, Liv. You could never be in the Olympics – you're rubbish at sport,' Isaac says, turning to look at me as if I am an idiot. That's another thing about my brother that can be annoying – he is *very* literal.

We cross the road and head in the direction of the corner shop.

'Can't wait, can't wait,' chants Isaac as we get closer.

I can see a group of boys from my school coming towards us and put my hand on Isaac's back, rubbing gently in a circle. He gets nervous when he sees other boys his age – he's had some horrible experiences and he's always worried that it'll happen again.

'When we get in the shop, I'll fetch the milk and you can go and choose your magazine,' I say to him, trying to distract his attention from the boys who are nearly next to us.

Isaac turns to me in surprise.

'I don't need to *choose*, Liv – I know which magazine I'm getting. It's the one I always get, every first Saturday of the month. It's called *How Stuff Works*. I thought you knew that.' His voice is incredulous and a bit hurt, but it's worked. The boys are past us now and I can stop rubbing his back.

'Sorry, Isaac – I *do* know that – silly me, hey?' I grin at him and he smiles back. Isaac may be quite irritating in lots of ways but he doesn't hold a grudge. We're nearly at the shop now and Isaac starts striding ahead of me, desperate to get there. We walk past the gates to the park and I see a welly, lying on its side in a puddle. It's tiny – I reckon it's probably fallen off some little kid in a pram. It looks kind of cool, though, so I whip my camera out of my coat pocket and take a picture, zooming in close on the muddy water and the bright red welly. I love taking photographs like that – little snapshots that tell a story. Every time I look at the photo I'm going to imagine a small child having to hop everywhere so that he doesn't get a wet foot. Or maybe a lonely welly, abandoned and all alone, pining for its welly twin. Then I look up and see that Isaac is way ahead of me, so I shove my camera back in my pocket and run after him again, thinking that my brother is like my very own personal fitness instructor.

We get to the shop and I relax. This is Isaac's favourite thing to do and he would never, ever do anything that might mean he wasn't allowed to come and buy his magazine. His wall planner has a bright red star on the first Saturday of every month to remind him. I leave Isaac in the magazine aisle and head for the milk. Once I've got that I wander in the direction of the chocolate. Mum always lets me choose something that I like with the money that's left over and today I feel like taking my time and really getting my money's worth.

The first sign that something is wrong is when I hear the shop lady shouting.

'Stop that at once! What on earth do you think you're doing?'

I look up and my heart sinks. She's heading down the magazine aisle – the aisle where I left Isaac. I drop the milk and run round the corner, reaching Isaac at the same time that she does.

My brother is sitting on the floor of the shop, grabbing magazines frantically off the shelf and throwing them to one side. He's not saying anything at the moment, just whispering under his breath.

'You can't behave like that in here! What are you playing at? *Stop that this instant!*' screams the shop lady.

'Don't yell at him,' I tell her and sink down on the floor next to Isaac.

'Talk to me – tell me what's wrong,' I say to him gently.

'It's all wrong, Liv, all wrong,' mutters Isaac, still yanking magazines out of the rack and on to the floor.

'Just be calm and tell me what it is,' I say, keeping my voice quiet. I can see a crowd gathering at the end of the aisle, trying to see what's going on.

'I'll give him calm!' shrieks the shop lady. 'Get out now – and I'll expect you to pay for the damages.'

She takes a step towards Isaac.

'Don't touch him!' I shout at her but it's too late. She grabs his arm and tries to haul him up.

Big mistake.

Before she touched him, Isaac was upset but

I could have talked him round. By grabbing him she has made a huge error. Mum and Dad have taught Isaac lots of rules and one of them is that it's really important not to touch other people unless they say it's OK (he didn't used to get the difference between gentle and rough touching and he can be a bit, well, in your face, so we all make a point of letting him know if we want to give him a hug and we would *never* hurt him). The shop lady broke a big rule when she grabbed Isaac, and Isaac cannot stand people breaking the rules, which is fair enough when he has to work so hard to keep them.

To put it simply, he goes ballistic.

Instead of throwing the magazines, he starts ripping them up and doing this high-pitched scream that goes right through you. People say that the sound of nails on a blackboard makes them shiver – that sound has nothing on Isaac when he's really going for it.

The shop lady backs right off, which should have been a relief, except I am trying to figure out how to get Isaac out of the shop without us both being arrested. I can hear lots of tutting from the onlookers and I really want to swear at them, but

Mum says not to sink to their level and that they don't understand.

'Isaac, it's OK, it's all right. We'll go home and Mum will sort it out,' I say, trying to keep my voice steady. If Isaac knows that you're freaked out it just makes him worse. 'Let's go home, Isaac. Leave all this here. Turn it around now – make a good choice.'

I am running out of things to say and am just pulling my mobile phone out of my pocket to ring Mum when Isaac stops screaming.

The silence is as surprising as the noise had been. I look at him and see huge tears dripping down his face as he starts sobbing, great big sobs that make him breathe in air in huge gulps. Right now, my big brother looks about five years old.

I take hold of his hand and start leading him down the aisle, past all the nosy shoppers who step aside as if we're contagious.

'Honestly, what a way to carry on!' tuts one old bag.

'Well, he's got a lifetime ban from this shop,' whines the shop lady. 'He's probably on drugs.'

I've had enough. I know that Mum says we shouldn't have to explain about Isaac to anyone, but these people are judging him in a way that I can't bear – not when they've all been happy to stand and gawp and act as if they've never made a wrong decision in their lives.

'If you must know, he's got Asperger's Syndrome,' I inform the tutting woman and the shop lady. 'He doesn't always see things the way that you might see them. Sometimes things get a bit much for him but he never means to cause any trouble. He can't help it – and something must have upset him.'

The shop lady goes a bit red in the face and the other shoppers melt back into the shop – amazing how people aren't so interested when they feel a bit guilty.

'I'll get my mum or dad to ring you up and you can tell them all about how much they owe you. Perhaps you can explain the lifetime ban to them too.'

I turn to the door and pull Isaac with me, my heart beating so fast that I think it might come right out of my chest. We walk down the road, me ignoring the curious looks of people walking past and rubbing Isaac's back so hard that he winces and pulls away.

After a few minutes I feel calm enough to speak

to him, although I don't actually want to look at him right now.

'Care to explain that little drama then?' I ask, my voice sounding harsh even to my own ears. 'Seriously? It mattered that much to you, did it? I mean, is it actually too much to ask that you behave like everybody else *just for once*? Because, maybe I'm massively selfish, but I would really like to go out of the house occasionally and not have people stare at me because you're doing something weird. Why me, Isaac? Why do I have to put up with this all the time? It's so unfair . . .'

I stomp along, not even caring for a moment whether Isaac is behind me or not. I can't stop thinking about the people in the shop – and everyone else who has ever ground to a halt and just stood there, watching our family try to do normal things like everyone else but usually messing it up. I try to tell myself that I don't care, that Isaac's my brother and I'm not embarrassed – but sometimes, I really am.

I stop, and turn round. Isaac is trailing behind me, looking a bit confused. He's stopped crying and is sniffing loudly, great big disgusting sniffs that yank the snot back up his nose. He has no idea why I am upset.

I sigh. 'What was wrong in the shop?'

'My magazine. It wasn't there. Somebody must have taken it, Liv, and that's not right.' He takes the tissue I am offering him and blows his nose loudly, startling a passing pigeon. 'It's *my* magazine and somebody took it. They didn't ask me if they could have it and that's breaking one of the rules.'

He hands the tissue back to me. I scrunch it up and put it in my coat pocket, making a mental note to get Mum to remove it and wash my coat before I next wear it.

There is no point trying to tell Isaac that nobody has stolen his magazine. Not up to me, anyway – that's Mum and Dad's job. My only responsibility is getting him home safely, preferably before my stupid, lame coat actually dissolves in the rain.

'Where's my milk?' asks Mum when we finally get through the front door.

Oh yeah – the milk. The milk that I dropped on the floor when I raced to rescue Isaac. I think about how I felt in the shop and how scared I was that Mum wasn't there to handle Isaac – and the relief of having actually got him home in one piece suddenly hits me and I start laughing hysterically. By the time I have calmed down she has cleaned up Isaac's face, got the gist of what has happened from him, promised to drive him into town later to buy his magazine from a bigger shop that won't have sold out and brought me a calming bar of chocolate. Then she sits down on the sofa next to me and lets me cry for a bit. She lets me moan about what a nightmare it is, having to protect Isaac all the time, and she doesn't say a word. She only stops me when I start going on about his rules.

'His stupid, pointless rules. They cause more trouble than they're worth. Life doesn't have rules for everything – I don't think we should keep telling him that it does.'

'You're wrong, Liv,' says Mum. 'There are rules for every situation you will ever find yourself in. The problems come when you don't understand what those rules are. Isaac needs us to explain the rules to him in a really clear way – your rules can be less clear but they're still there and they're still just as important.' She bends over and kisses me on the forehead. 'Now, I'm going to take Isaac to get his magazine because I promised, and that's one rule that definitely cannot be broken. However, the rule about you not watching TV before your room is tidy is slightly more flexible!'

I sink back into the sofa and listen to the sounds

of Mum and Isaac getting ready to go out. Dad is pottering around in the kitchen and has already stuck his head through the door to tell me that, in honour of my awesome little-sister skills, he is cooking up a Mexican feast of all my favourite foods. And that he is proud of me. I think that really, even though my family cause me more than my fair share of embarrassment and humiliation, I wouldn't change them for anything.

Eleven Weeks
Before

I'm mooching around the garden trying to find something interesting to snap with my camera. I'm kind of obsessed with photographs. I love the way that they're memory evidence, total proof that you saw something or did something or were just *there*. It's not actually raining for a change, and I'm starting to enjoy myself when Mum marches out through the kitchen door. She has that look of determination that I know so well – and I know there is no point in trying to (a) escape from her or (b) argue my way out of whatever it is that she wants me to do.

'Right, come on, Liv, let's get moving.'

She says this as if we have plans, as if I have the foggiest idea of what she's going on about.

I stare at her blankly.

'Chop chop – I haven't got all day.'

She turns round and walks back towards the house and then, sensing that I haven't moved, spins back to look at me.

To be perfectly honest, I'm not in the mood for this. I've had a rubbish day at school. I thought I'd got away with it – however, it turns out that gossip moves slowly but steadily through our school and Moronic Louise Phillips had obviously just heard all about my excruciating experience in Hair & Things. She spent the whole day making stupid comments about how cool it is to be able to wear earrings, and flicking her hair about so that everyone could admire her obviously fake gold hoops. The only good bit was when Mr Jackson, our science teacher, threatened to confiscate them if she ever wore them to school again. I tried to ignore her but she has one of those voices that really gets in your head and buzzes about, like an irritating insect.

I probably shouldn't have called her a liar, though. I *know* it's better to just let her get on with it and that confronting her only makes her worse, but I couldn't just stand there and let her talk down about Mum.

'My mum's so cool,' she said. 'Not like your mum at all. Honestly, Liv – how do you cope having such a control freak for a mother?' Her ridiculous friends all sniggered and I could feel Alice pulling my arm and trying to walk us away. My blood was boiling, though. I mean, yeah – my mum can be a total nightmare sometimes, but that's for me to say, not Moronic Louise.

'Actually,' she carried on, 'my mum said that I can get my nose pierced and that as soon as I'm eighteen she'll take me to get a tattoo!' Her friends all 'oohed' and 'ahhed' like the pathetic hangers-on that they are.

'What will you have done?' asked Molly, Louise's second-in-command.

That's when I should have walked away. But I didn't and the sound of Moronic Louise debating whether she'd look cuter with a tattoo of a rose, or a tattoo of her puppy, made me want to throw up. So I volunteered my own suggestion – that she was a total liar and there's no way that her mum would let her do that. I said that I thought she'd look particularly striking with the letters M-O-R-O-N tattooed across her forehead. And then I offered to save her time and money by doing it myself with a biro.

She was obviously not mad keen on my idea, or particularly pleased that some of the boys in our class overheard me and laughed. A lot. So it was probably my own fault that she decided it'd be oh-so-hilarious to tell Ben that I fancy him. Actually, I really do, but as he started making retching noises and rolling his eyes at his mates, I had to pretend it was the most disgusting thing I'd ever heard and that 'I wouldn't go out with *him* if aliens had inhabited earth and he was my only hope of survival'. So that's the end of that. Thanks, Louise.

Anyway, Mum has been in a really foul mood all week. She keeps snapping at Dad for coming home late and then on Wednesday, *she* didn't come back from work until really late and I missed going to Guides. She didn't even tell me that she'd be late – I could have been really worried. Alice said Guides was a total laugh and they made peppermint creams, but they wouldn't set and were all runny and went everywhere, and Sophie (chief, most-important, bow-down-before-her, Head Guider) went mad and it was hysterical.

So I am not particularly interested in whatever dumb activity Mum may have dreamt up for me, especially as she seems to have an allergic reaction to the sight of me chilling out and doing my own thing.

'Liv, I'm serious – move yourself right now.

Don't make me count to five like you're four years old!'

This is a bit rich coming from a woman who seems to believe that the clocks all stopped when I became a toddler and that I haven't actually matured since.

'I'm busy, Mum. What is it?' I whine, ever hopeful that she'll go away and leave me alone.

'Busy! Doing what, may I ask?'

No, actually, you may not . . . I might not look like I'm doing very much but there's a lot of thinking going on here.

'Could it be that you're busy doing your homework? Or frantically tidying your bedroom? Or maybe working on a plan for worldwide peace and harmony?' My mother can be very sarcastic. 'Hmm, I thought not – so clean that mud off your trainers, get inside, wash your hands *thoroughly* and meet me in the kitchen in three minutes. You can take your photos later.'

She strides back inside, a mother on a mission, and I grudgingly start to move. That's another thing about my mum. If she issues you with a direct instruction, she expects you to comply with it *exactly* – and she is very precise about what she expects. I mean, why three minutes? Anyone else would have said 'a few minutes' or 'when you've washed your hands', but not her. She'll have planned just how long I can reasonably be expected to take to carry out her demands, and probably added thirty seconds for the sulking part where I pretend that I'm not going to do what she's asked.

Which is what I'm doing now and – oops – time's up, so I'd better get a wriggle on. No point in annoying her. Who knows, maybe she wants to take me shopping or to the cinema or something else cool. She didn't actually say what it was she wanted me for, did she?

Precisely thirty-eight minutes later and I am not happily browsing this season's latest look, nor am I settling down with a bucket of toffee popcorn to watch a film.

No – I am standing at the work surface in our kitchen, chopping a red pepper and listening to Mum explain why, if need be, man (or woman) can live on spaghetti Bolognese alone.

For some reason, known only to her, it is utterly crucial that I learn how to concoct this wondrous dish *today*. This task cannot wait until a rainy day, or indeed a day when I actually feel like touching squirmy, wormy strands of beef (sometime never).

Mum has decided that I need to learn to cook now and that she is the one best equipped to teach me – which is bizarre, cos Mum hates cooking and is actually an awful cook.

I'm not being mean here, or saying anything I wouldn't say to her face. She knows how bad her food is and she's as happy as the rest of us on the days that Dad gets back from work early enough to cook supper. So this lesson is a bit inappropriate and fairly unnecessary. I have no intention of ever needing to know how to cook. When I'm working in my high-powered job I'll just get takeaways, or maybe marry someone who's a good cook. Sorted.

'The thing is, Liv, a meal like this can provide all the necessary nutrients needed for a healthy lifestyle. If you make sure that you buy lean meat and throw some extra vegetables in and serve it with grated cheese, you're basically covered.'

'That's great, Mum.' I keep chopping my pepper. Best to humour her when she's like this.

'And I've chosen this meal to teach you because – *guess what*!'

'I don't know, Mum – what?'

'It isn't just a spaghetti Bolognese!'

'*No!* What else could it possibly be? A flat-screen TV? A new mobile phone? Wait – I've got it! A buy-one-get-one-free voucher for a pizza! Something I'd actually be interested in?'

'Less cheek from you, madam, thank you! No, what I was *about* to say was that this meal can be used as a pasta sauce or with baked potatoes, or you can add some kidney beans for an instant chilli con carne. It's extremely versatile and you'll thank me one day for sharing my culinary wisdom with you!' Mum tries to swat me with the tea towel and I dodge out of the way, giggling. She starts laughing too, and for the next few minutes we chop our vegetables together and I tell her about the French test I aced today.

The pepper has been chopped into the tiniest pieces possible (Isaac hates peppers and always picks them out of his food, so I am working hard to make this extra difficult for him).

'Shall I put this in the pan now?' I ask, thrusting the fruits (or vegetables) of my labour in front of her.

Mum looks up and I see a tear dripping silently down her cheek, followed by another. She sees me looking and quickly brushes them away.

'Mum?' I put my hand on her arm. 'Are you *crying*?'

She shrugs me off with a laugh.

'Don't be so ridiculous, Liv! I'm chopping onions – it always makes my eyes water. Not sure why, must be to do with oniony chemicals. Or something. We could Google it. What do you think – have you learnt about onions in school?'

My mother is rambling. I keep on looking at her, searching her face for evidence of more tears, but they seem to have dried up – which is funny because now she's chopping onions as if her life depended on it.

'Get the olive oil out of the cupboard and bring it over here,' she says, not looking at me. I do what she tells me, feeling worried but not really sure why.

'Now just slosh a bit in this pan.' Mum points to a pan on top of the stove and I take the lid off the oil.

'Does it actually say "slosh" in the recipe book?' I ask her.

'What recipe book?' answers Mum, and she finally looks across at me and grins. I stifle a groan. This is *not* good news. Mum's experimental cooking is never a success.

I follow her instructions, although there's a good chance that when she said 'slosh' she didn't mean half the bottle. She gets me to turn on the hob and then hovers next to me while I heat up the oil, acting like I might set myself on fire at any moment. I tell her that I have used a stove before, at school, but she still stays right next to me.

Soon the smell of frying onions fills the kitchen and I sniff deeply. I love that smell – it always makes me think about carnivals and fairs and bonfires and barbecues. Hot dogs and burgers and eating outdoors. It reminds me of staying up late and half falling asleep, cuddled up to Mum. We tip the beef into the pan and I stir it, watching as the disgusting pink strands change colour. Then Mum says that it doesn't really matter what goes in – that the chef gets to choose and it can be different every time. I add the peppers and some tins of chopped tomatoes and give everything a good stir. That was actually quite easy. I reckon I could make spag Bol on my own, no problem. Not sure why Mum made such a big deal of it.

Mum gathers up the empty tins and starts to tidy the kitchen. There's a surprising amount of mess – yet another reason for just ordering a takeaway, in my opinion.

'Everything's sorted here. You get back to your photos, sweetheart! Good job with the chopping –

try to remember everything I showed you, won't you?' she says.

I take off the ridiculous apron that she made me wear and start to head back into the garden, but something makes me pause. Seeing me stop, Mum dashes over and gives me a huge hug – the sort of hug that starts to feel uncomfortable because the hugger is holding the huggee so tightly that the huggee thinks they might actually suffocate and end up with *Olivia Ellis, Hugged To Death, aged eleven and a half years* on their gravestone.

After what feels like a lifetime she lets go and heads back to the tidying up, and I go outside. I thought that I wanted to relax and get a bit of peace, but it's suddenly really cold and I don't feel like being on my own.

I think about what just happened. Was Mum crying? The thing is, I've seen Mum cry loads but it's always noisy and a bit dramatic, and usually sparked by a sad film that she seems to think is actually about her. She did cry once on her birthday when she and Dad had agreed a £10 budget and he spent it all in Oxfam, buying about a million rubbish books that nobody wanted, especially not her (which was what she yelled at him in between sobbing that it was her worst birthday *ever*) – but then he took her out shopping for new boots and a meal, so it all ended up OK and they even laugh about it now.

The point is that I have never, ever seen my mum cry quietly and I have never heard her deny that she is crying. She likes to wear her emotions openly like badges and doesn't really do angst – she always says there's no point in being miserable unless everyone knows that you're miserable cos then they can do something about it . . .

I decide that, probably, there're a few things that I could learn about how to boil spaghetti, so it's not a bad idea to go back inside and help Mum out with the rest of the supper. There's a darkness in the garden that I didn't notice before and the kitchen suddenly seems like a good place to hang out.

There's more of a chance that supper will actually be edible if I go and help, anyway. And I'm feeling a bit odd inside, like something is wrong somewhere, and that hanging out with Mum might make me feel OK again.

Ten Weeks
Before

Today has been the best day *ever*. I thought it was going to be a bit of a boring weekend, but Mum woke me up this morning while Isaac and Dad were still asleep and told me to get dressed as quickly as possible cos we were having a day out. She made me be really quiet so that I didn't wake Isaac up. I wanted to tell her that she had no worries on that account – I'd gone to the loo at 3 a.m. and he was still playing games on his PlayStation so it was unlikely that he'd be awake much before lunchtime – but I didn't want to ruin her good mood so I said nothing.

Then, when we were in the car, she said that we were going to spend the day shopping – and not just in town but somewhere bigger with proper shops and a pizza restaurant and *everything*!

I cannot believe the cool stuff that Mum bought

me today. It's as if every birthday I'm ever going to have came at the same time. We started off looking for clothes and she didn't get distracted once – normally we start off shopping for me but she gets sidetracked with stuff that she wants and then, just when I'm thinking it's my turn, she realizes that the car park ticket is about to run out and we have to sprint back to the car before the ticket warden gives Mum yet another fine.

Today, though, we went into my favourite ever clothes shop and she bought me a pair of new jeans and a cool pair of combat trousers and then, when I saw a super-awesome tube top in neon orange, she just picked it up and added it to the pile, cool as a cucumber! She didn't even look at the price.

Then we bought loads of T-shirts and a couple of sweatshirts for me – I guess she must think I'll need them and I'm not complaining. Everything was a bit big, but Mum says I'll grow into it all and it's better to buy larger now so that I don't need new clothes for a while.

The only embarrassing part of the day was when she dragged me into the massive department store next to the bank. I was really in the swing of shopping by now, carrier bags in both hands, and

I thought that maybe she wanted to get us lunch or something. But, instead, we went upstairs to the underwear department where she stocked up with about a year's supply of knickers and socks and then, horror of horrors, forced me into a changing room and told me to strip.

'It's a very momentous day, darling – buying your first bra!' said Mum, while taking my bags from me and putting them down in the corner of the huge cubicle.

Now, I'm not usually shy and while I was loving all the attention that Mum was giving me, I can tell you, one hundred per cent truthfully, that I have *absolutely, definitely* no use for a bra of any kind. My crop tops are fine. All the girls will laugh themselves silly if I turn up in the changing rooms wearing an actual bra – I'll look like a total try-hard. I did my best to convey this message to Mum in a simple but efficient manner.

'No way, Mum – are you out of your mind?' I said, while crossing my arms across my front and backing away from her.

'There's nothing to worry about, Liv – think of it as part of your journey into womanhood!' Mum said. 'Come on now – coat off. That nice lady will be in with her tape measure in a moment.'

Oh, great. Totally fantastic. Not only was I going to have the indignity of Mum grinning away like a maniac, I'd have to cope with some old woman seeing me in all my non-glory.

'Are we all ready in there?' called the old woman.

'One moment, please!' called back Mum chirpily, while hissing at me to 'take that coat off and stop behaving like a big ninny'.

Ninny? What is a ninny anyway?

'All ready for you now!' she chirruped to the shop lady, who parted the curtains as enthusiastically as Moses parting the Red Sea and sailed into my cubicle.

'Aahh – first bra, is it?' she cooed.

The sight of me cowering in the corner, red as a tomato, must have given her a clue.

'Oh, I love it when the young girls come in with their mums. Like a rite of passage, it is! Come on now, lovely – arms out to the side and stand here where I can measure you.'

'Hope your tape measure has negative numbers,' I mumbled, but she and Mum were too busy chattering about the thrill of buying your first womanly undergarments to hear me.

Bra Lady got to work, wrapping the tape measure round my non-existent chest and squinting to read the result. I wanted to reassure her that she wasn't losing her eyesight – my chest really *is* that small, but the way Mum was looking at me (a combination of pride, love and threat) stopped me saying anything. Turns out that I didn't need to.

'She's quite ... uhhm ... petite, dear,' she said, turning to Mum. 'I think it might be better to wait another six months and come back then, perhaps when she's grown a bit more. Or maybe get her a training bra. They're quite popular with the younger girls.'

'No, I'd rather we got it now,' smiled Mum. Well, her mouth was smiling but her eyes were giving out quite a different message altogether.

'If you're sure, dear,' agreed Bra Lady, turning back to me and tweaking the tape measure. 'It's just that she is incredibly tiny and we don't stock proper bras in this size. I don't think we actually make them this small. Never mind, lovey – I'll find you the smallest one we've got and you'll grow into it eventually.'

Bra Lady breezed back out of the cubicle. I grabbed my T-shirt and started pulling it over my head, desperate to get out of there.

'Come on, Mum – let's go,' I said, but Mum just stood there, looking at me with a funny expression on her face. 'Mum! You heard her. I don't even need a bra yet. It'll be a complete waste of money.'

I was sure that'd get her to see sense. Mum hates wasting money and she's always going on about watching the pennies. She gave her head a little shake and then picked up her bag.

'Oh, Liv, this was a daft idea. I just really wanted to do this with you. I was being silly – I'm sorry, sweetheart.'

She looked so sad for a moment and I couldn't work out why our day suddenly didn't feel so good. I wondered if I'd done something wrong; I suppose I did make a bit of a fuss about getting measured.

'I don't mind if you want to buy me a bra, Mum, but I don't want to wear it for school yet, that's all. And it was embarrassing when that lady came in.'

Mum looked at me again and smiled. 'I wasn't thinking about it properly. We can still do this, but we don't need anyone to help us. It'll be lots more fun on our own, you'll see. Hurry up, coat on, and let's go!'

And you know what? Mum was right. She was determined that I needed to buy a bra and that, even if it didn't fit me now, I'd 'definitely need it in the next year so it isn't a waste of money'. Personally,

I think she's a bit deluded in her predictions – can't see me needing one in the next five years, but it was fun in the end. She found Bra Lady and thanked her for her help, and then we went to some amazing shops and chose tiny bras that even I have to admit are pretty cool. I'm quite looking forward to being old enough to wear them, but for now they're in my cupboard, all wrapped up in gorgeous tissue paper.

After underwear shopping Mum was exhausted and we went to get a pizza for lunch (I didn't even have to beg her!). And after that was the best bit. Mum took me down a street that I hadn't been to before and led me into a real-life tattoo parlour! No, don't worry – I didn't get a tattoo (she hasn't gone officially insane, just a bit loopy). It's way better than that. I am now the proud owner of a pair of pierced ears! Mum reckons that tattoo parlours have to keep a good reputation and can't afford to be shoddy over customer hygiene, so she'd rung them up and had a good chat, and they'd told her all about the certificates they have to get to show that they're a safe place – then she'd made me an appointment.

I *love, love, love* my ears! They've got cute little studs in at the moment but in six weeks I can change them, and Mum took me straight from getting them done to buy some dangly ones for when I can wear them! Not for school, she said, but I can wear them at weekends. They're totally gorgeous – long silver strands that swoosh together and make a tinkling sound. I love them!

Mum was tired again after all the excitement so we went for a coffee and a sandwich. And then we went to the cinema. Just us two – not with Dad and Isaac. Can't remember the last time we did that. I spent most of the time twiddling my earrings until Mum told me to stop and that I'd infect my ears with nasty germs.

I was worn out on the way home but *so* happy! When we got back, I showed Dad my new ears and went straight up to bed. I cleaned my teeth and then realized that I'd left my new clothes downstairs so I went down to fetch them. I could hear Dad before I'd even got to the end of the hall.

'I'm *not* trying to spoil things, Rachel. I'm just worried, that's all.'

I could hear Mum crashing things about in the sink. 'We had a great day, Dan – can't that be enough?'

'It's not enough and you know it. You can't buy

her off. Money is not going to make everything OK for her, you know that. She needs to be told the truth and she needs to know it soon.'

There was a bigger crash as if something had fallen (or been thrown) and then the sound of Mum yelling.

'Of course I know, you idiot, but maybe it's all I've got to give right now – have you thought of that? The truth isn't going to make this OK, is it? I'm lying awake at nights wondering how to explain it to her. And as for helping Isaac make sense of it, well . . .'

Everything went quiet for a moment and then I could hear muffled sobbing.

I backtracked along the hall, past the photos of Isaac and me as babies, and Aunt Leah graduating from university, and Mum and Dad lying on a beach somewhere exotic. I backed up the stairs, never taking my eyes off the kitchen door, which stayed shut. Only when I reached the landing did I dare to turn and run as quickly as possible to my bedroom door, which I slammed shut behind me before throwing myself on the bed. I can't believe it. Not *my* mum and dad? I knew something was wrong but what I've just heard confirms my worst suspicions.

They must be getting a divorce and Mum is trying to figure out how to tell me.

Where will we live? Isaac couldn't cope with moving house. What if they make us choose who we want to stay with? How can they be so *selfish* – I bet they haven't thought about us at all.

Nine Weeks
Before

My world is, quite literally, falling apart.

Who could have guessed that *my* family would end up part of a national statistic? I mean, maybe I've always taken it for granted, but I thought we were a happy family. Sure, Mum and Dad get mad at each other now and then, but they always seem to make friends pretty quickly and they love doing things together. At the end of each day, the thing they like best is sitting at our kitchen table and telling each other about everything they've been up to and making plans for the next weekend or school holiday.

I just don't understand how it could have got so bad without me realizing.

I'm walking to school with Alice and I've decided to tell her about it – but not before swearing her to secrecy. She's sympathetic, but doesn't seem to understand how massive this is for me.

'It's not all bad, you know. My dad spends far more time with me now than he used to when he lived with us. And he actually tries to be nice to me now – I guess he's worried I'll refuse to see him or something!' she laughs, giving my arm a squeeze.

'But my dad is nice to me already, and I see loads of him,' I moan. I'm thinking that if she starts talking about two sets of Christmas and birthday presents that I might actually scream.

'And I know everyone says it – but it's true – I do get more presents at Christmas and they're actually things that I want!' says Alice.

I grit my teeth and remind myself that I need Alice right now, and that yelling at her is not going to help. It's not *her* fault that my stupid parents can't be happy with what they've got and seem to feel the need to ruin my life. So selfish.

'Although it does seem a bit weird that they've not told you yet,' Alice comments.

'I *know*! So typical of my family – don't tell Liv anything. Probably think I'll make a big fuss and upset everyone!'

'Well, won't you?' grins Alice as we round the corner to the school gates.

It's early spring, and the daffodils are everywhere, their yellow bonnet heads gently swaying in the early morning breeze. I like daffodils, but my favourite flowers are dandelions – I've got loads of photos that I've taken of them, some when they've got their flowers and others with a head full of seeds. Mum always laughs at me and says that they're weeds and nobody chooses dandelions as their favourite – but I like their determination, growing everywhere, even in among all the rubbish. They're a bit like finding a piece of treasure in an unlikely place and they always make me feel happy.

Not any more, though, I think as I stomp past a clump growing out from behind the bin by the bus stop. Now they'll remind me of the spring I discovered that my parents wanted to destroy my family. Thanks a lot, Mum and Dad. We might not be the perfect family but I always thought we were OK. Now they're going to rip everything apart before I've had a chance to do half the things I wanted to do. I can kiss my life's dream of going to Disneyland goodbye, that's for sure. Once they start splitting everything up and paying for two

49

homes instead of one, there'll be no money for holidays. I've seen it on TV – I know all about it.

'Yes, I *will* make a fuss, and so will Isaac when they actually have the courage to tell him. Somebody has to fight for this family and it looks like it'll have to be me.' I link arms with Alice and march into school, half hoping that Moronic Louise will have the sense to stay away from me today, and half hoping that she gives me a reason to deal with her, once and for all.

My day passes in the usual, boring blur that is school. I must be giving out some serious 'keep away' vibes because Moronic Louise doesn't come anywhere near me. In fact, I hardly talk to anyone all day. I can't be bothered to look for Alice at lunchtime – instead I creep into the library and find a chair in the corner where nobody can see me unless they come looking. I sneak bites from my sandwich when I can hear that the librarian is busy on the other side of the room, and sink into the world of my book. It's better than my real world.

Now I'm home and the only thing that I want to do is slump in front of the television. On my own. Without any annoying brothers doing their absolute best to ruin my peace.

No chance in this house, though. Isaac has

slammed through the door, made a ton of noise in the kitchen getting a snack and is now standing in front of me, blocking my view of the TV and munching a piece of toast, *very loudly*.

I try ignoring him. He just carries on, standing and munching. So I take it to the next level and give him my best 'death stare'. Lesser mortals have been known to pass out with terror when subjected to this look – but not Isaac. He doesn't even shake.

'Isaac, move,' I tell him.

'Have you seen my Pokemon cards?' he says.

'No.' My voice is cold and sharp – I want to be left alone, just for a few minutes.

'They're missing,' Isaac says.

'Not interested. Move.'

'I can't find them.'

'Talk to the hand, Isaac.'

Isaac looks at me for a moment and I think he's finally got the message. He frowns and then holds his hand up in the air in front of him.

'Hand – where are my Pokemon cards?' he asks it.

I explode. He has finally pushed my last button and I've had enough.

'You are *not* stupid, Isaac! Take the hint! I don't want to talk to you, OK? Go away.'

I sink back into the sofa, already regretting my outburst, but wishing with every bit of me that, just for once, Isaac could think about someone other than himself.

Isaac takes a last bite of his toast, crumbs dropping on to the carpet as he wipes his hands together, careful to make sure that no toast remains on his fingers.

'And I don't want to talk to you, Liv. I just want to know where my Pokemon cards are.' He is looking at a spot on the wall above my head and I know that I've confused him. That he has no idea what he's done wrong. I shake my head to let him know that I can't help him and he walks away. I follow him with my eyes and see Mum, leaning in the doorway to the kitchen. She smiles at Isaac as he goes past and then looks at me.

'Bad day?' she asks.

'You have no idea,' I mutter. I don't particularly want to talk to her either, not when she's planning on tearing our family apart.

'Tell me about it?' she says, but I shake my head at her too. She turns to leave.

'It wasn't my fault,' I blurt out, and she stops and turns back to me, eyebrows raised in a question. 'Just now, with Isaac – it wasn't my fault. Anyone else would have known to leave me alone. It's not a crime to need a bit of space now and again.'

'But Isaac isn't "anyone else", is he?' says Mum. 'He doesn't understand what you want unless you tell him, Liv. You know that.'

'Great,' I say, scowling. 'So we just have to put up with it, do we, for the rest of our lives? We just accept that Isaac needs everything spelling out for him – even how the rest of us are feeling?'

'Particularly how the rest of us are feeling,' says Mum. 'Think how much we communicate using our faces and our bodies, Liv. The minute I walked in here I could tell that you were cross, and that something's bothering you. You didn't have to tell me in words – it was clear from the way you were frowning and crossing your arms. It was obvious from the way your lips were squeezed together. But Isaac can't read that language. It's like asking you to talk to someone who only speaks Bulgarian. It'd be really hard.'

I sit up a bit straighter, thinking about what Mum is saying.

'I get all that, Mum – really I do. But can't he learn to "read" how we're feeling? He's learnt to do a whole heap of other stuff, so why can't he just learn to look at people's faces and figure out how they're feeling.'

Mum smiles at me. 'He can, but he needs some help. Don't you remember, we had those drawings of faces that we used to show him? He was great at remembering what the faces were *supposed* to mean – he just found it a bit trickier to relate that to real, live people. Dad and I have been meaning to try something else, but there's been a lot of other stuff happening lately and we haven't got round to it. I will, I promise, Liv. But in the meantime, try to be patient with him. We're asking a lot of him and it isn't going to happen overnight.'

I stand up. I don't want this conversation carrying on, not if she's going to start talking about the 'other stuff' that's been going on around here. Anyway, I've just had a brilliant idea for helping Isaac and I can get started on it straight away.

'Don't worry,' I tell Mum. 'I can help him. I reckon I've got a great plan.'

Mum looks at me and for a second I think she's about to burst into tears. Then she takes a few steps towards me and pulls me into a hug.

'Thank you, Liv,' she whispers. 'Isaac is really going to need you on his team. I'm so proud of you, the way you look out for him.'

'He's my brother,' I say, pulling away from her. 'That's what families do, isn't it – look out for each other?'

I run up the stairs, taking them two at a time, and dash into my room. My camera is on my desk and I grab it. It's old and not great but it'll do the job. I head across the hall to Isaac's room. His door is half open so I give a quick knock and stick my head round. Isaac is sitting cross-legged on his bed, Pokemon cards spread out all around him. He is smiling.

'You found them then?' I say.

He looks up at me and grins, and I fire off a quick shot, the flash of the camera making him blink.

'What was that?' he asks.

'That was "happy",' I tell him, and then I walk downstairs with the hope of seeing Mum or Dad demonstrating an emotion that I can capture on camera.

Eight Weeks
Before

I'm still plucking up the courage to talk to Mum and Dad about them splitting up. I haven't done it yet because (a) they don't seem to be arguing any more, and (b) something massively momentous has happened.

I was sitting in my science class this afternoon with Alice, pretending to understand what Mr Jackson had asked us to do. I know it had something to do with a Bunsen burner and some liquid, but other than that it was a complete mystery to me. Alice wasn't being much help either cos she was busy trying to finish her French homework, which was due in next period – Madame Dupont is not universally known for her tolerance and compassion when her pupils are late with homework. You could show her video evidence of your dog *literally* eating your French verbs and she would still look stony-faced and give you a detention slip.

I had a quick glance over my shoulder to the bench behind me, where Ben and Jack were sitting, to see if I could get any clues about what to do. And that's when it happened. Ben smiled at me! It was only a little smile and he looked away straight afterwards, but it was still a smile – just for me!

That smile made today the best science lesson *ever*. Even when Mr Jackson stormed over to our bench and started yelling at us and asking why we hadn't actually done anything purposeful all lesson. Even when I could see Moronic Louise nudging her equally stupid friend and sniggering at me. Even when Alice was a bit fed up with me for not attempting to keep us out of trouble and under the radar with Mr Jackson. All I could do was look kindly at my fellow classmates and hug the memory of that smile to myself.

Alice instantly forgave me when we got out of science and I told her why I'd been acting so strangely. She understood completely that I could not be expected to focus on the mundanities of the science national curriculum while forces of nature were aligning the stars that would bring Ben and me together. Or something like that.

I float home after school and drift into the kitchen. And of course Mum can tell that something is up.

'Had a good day, Liv?' she asks, peering at me over the top of her reading glasses.

'S'all right, I s'pose,' I mumble back, trying to play it cool and pretending to be absorbed in the back of the newspaper that she's reading.

'OK – spill!' she says, folding up the paper and putting it on the table. 'We both know you want to tell me something.'

I think for a moment. Should I tell her? I'm pretty sure she'll get why I'm excited – but all of a sudden I feel a bit embarrassed about actually saying the words. My camera is lying on the kitchen table where I left it this morning and I pick it up, glad to have something to do with my hands while I think about what to say.

'I know something's going on, Olivia Ellis.' Mum leans forward and rests on her elbows, looking me in the eye.

'Maybe,' I say, grinning inside. I actually do want to tell her but it's kind of fun, making her wait like this.

'You know you're going to tell me anyway, so get on with it!' Mum has utterly no patience and she won't take no for an answer. Which is actually pretty cool most of the time – I hardly ever want to keep things from her and she often has good advice (sometimes she has some terrible advice too, so I just ignore her on those occasions). I aim the camera at her face and push the button. Great – that's 'impatient' sorted for my Isaac project.

Then I plonk myself down in the chair opposite her and make sure I have her full attention.

'Ben smiled at me in science!' I lean back, smug in the knowledge that she will understand what an eventful day this is. She does not disappoint.

'OK – I can see why you're looking so excited! I presume we are talking about *the* Ben. Mr Gorgeous, Mr Sporty, Mr Clever?'

'Err – yes, Mum. How many Bens do you think I like?'

'Just checking,' she says. 'So, it's been a good day then?'

'The best!' I tell her. 'I really thought he didn't like me, but maybe I was wrong.'

'Earth to Liv – you were definitely wrong! Why on earth wouldn't he like you? I happen to know that you are extremely likeable. In fact, there would have to be something wrong with the poor boy if he *didn't* like you.'

'It was just a smile, Mum,' I say. 'He hasn't asked me out or anything.'

'Do you want him to?' asks Mum, smiling at me across the table.

I can feel a red blush spreading across my face as I think about all the reasons why I like Ben. I'm glad that Dad and Isaac aren't home yet – there is no way I could have this conversation if they were around.

'I'm not sure,' I whisper, suddenly feeling that Ben's smile could have meant just about anything. 'Yes – maybe – I don't know.'

'It's hard to know *what* to think about boys sometimes, isn't it?' says Mum and I look at her in surprise. What would she know about it? She's been married to Dad for fifteen years.

Mum laughs. I guess my face is telling her exactly what I'm thinking.

'Yes, Liv, believe it or not I was once your age. And I did like the occasional boy or two, or five. I do remember what it's like – and mostly I remember it being very confusing!' She takes hold of my hand. 'Ooh, cold hands!' Mum tucks my hand inside both of hers and rubs, warming my fingers.

'But it wasn't the same for you,' I tell her.

'No?' She moves on to my other hand.

'Everything's different these days. You and Dad are always saying that.'

'*Some* things are different,' she corrects. 'Other things will always be the same, and sometimes the only way to cope with things is by knowing that you are not the first person who has ever had to deal with a situation. And you will definitely not be the last.' She stops rubbing my hands and stares out of the window and it feels like I've lost her for a moment.

'Mum?' I say, and she snaps her head back towards me. 'I don't know what to do next.'

'You don't have to do anything special,' says Mum. 'Life is an adventure, Liv. Sometimes you just need to let it happen. Ben smiled at you – so smile back!'

I grin at her, feeling happy inside.

'I just need you to remember something really important,' Mum says, and I groan. Here it comes – the talk about keeping safe and behaving myself. I should have known that she wouldn't be able to resist giving me a lecture.

'I want you never to forget that I understand. I know how it feels. It's not always going to be easy for you to talk to me – but there's something I want to give you that I hope will help when you need reminding that you're not on your own.' Mum pushes back her chair and stands up.

'Get a snack and meet me upstairs in my room. Give me five minutes.' She leaves the kitchen and I'm left wondering what it is that she's talking about.

I make myself a drink and grab a biscuit from the pig tin. Isaac bought it for Mum for Mother's Day a few years ago. It's hideous actually, but Mum claims to love it. I think she only uses it cos she doesn't want to hurt Isaac's feelings and it was really a miracle that he bought her anything at all. He doesn't normally get the point of giving things to other people and I end up putting his name on whatever I've bought.

By the time I get upstairs, Mum is dragging a box out from under her bed and wiping an inch-thick layer of dust off the top.

'Ooh, what've you got there then? Family heirloom?' I say, throwing myself on the bed.

She hauls the box up and puts it down next to me. 'As close to a family heirloom as you're likely to get, so be impressed. Go on then, open it up!'

I have to admit, I am pretty excited. Ideas about

what might be inside the box are flying into my head – precious jewellery maybe, or a vintage summer dress that would make me irresistible to Ben. I yank open the lid and look inside.

'Books?' I say. 'And dusty, ancient ones too!'

'Hang on a minute, Liv – and less of the ancient if you don't mind. These aren't just any old books. They're my diaries from when I was young.'

Diaries, hey? My ears prick up at this and I start to feel a bit less disappointed. This could be hilarious – I bet Mum was a real goody-goody when she was a kid.

'Now, I'm not a world expert on anything but what I *do* know about is being an eleven-year-old girl. You don't have to read them all now, but I'm giving you these diaries to read whenever you think that nobody understands you.' Mum gives me a hug and starts to put the lid back on the box.

'Hey, let me have a look at them then,' I protest.

'Not a chance – not with me sitting here!' she laughs. 'Far too embarrassing. And I don't want you quoting the daft things I used to write about over the breakfast table, OK?'

She stands up and heads out of the room, stopping in the doorway and turning back to me.

'I'm going to the shed to pot up some plants – give me a yell if Dad phones. Put these in your room and read them when it feels like the right time. There're some pretty good rules for life in there, you know!'

I grin at her and pick up the box. Heading down the hall to my bedroom, I can hear Mum go downstairs, humming a tune that I vaguely remember.

I sit down on the window seat in my room. It's my favourite place to sit and think. If I close the curtains, then nobody can see me but I can look out and see everyone walking down the street outside our house. Today they're all rushing, heads bent against the driving rain that is pelting down and I'm glad to be inside.

I open up the box and pull out the first book. It looks really battered. The front cover is all creased and there's a stain that looks like it might once have been Weetabix. The title says *My Secret File: A Do-It-Yourself Dossier For Your Darkest Thoughts* and the price on the back says 95p. Crikey – it must be old then – you can't buy anything for 95p nowadays.

I open it up. The first page says *My Vital Statistics* and is full of fascinating (not!) facts about Mum, like she weighed 5 stone and had size 2 feet and brown eyes. Nothing remotely interesting here then. The next page is pretty similar – she'd written that her nickname was 'Rat' and that she was eight years and two months old. Her handwriting is *terrible*. I can't believe she has the nerve to have a go at me for writing sloppily. I can barely read what she's written in some places! I flick through and then find this page:

- MY PETS: Rover, my fish
- MY FAVOURITE BOOK: All the Famous Fives
- MOST USELESS THING I OWN: My Little Pony
- HOW MUCH POCKET MONEY I GET EACH WEEK: None
- HOW MUCH I'D LIKE TO GET: 50 pounds
- NOW A SERIOUS ANSWER: 10p
- IF I HAD £100 I'D BUY: A big doll
- FAVOURITE FOOD: Angel Delight and fish fingers
- BEST RECORDS: Culture Club, Adam and the Ants
- I AM TALENTED AT: Licking my nose

Hahaha! Mum had a My Little Pony! She is *always* telling me what a tomboy she was and that she spent all her time playing outside and climbing trees and helping out in the garden – and it turns out that all she actually wanted was a 'big doll'? What a waste of £100. If I had £100 I'd buy a new iPod or loads of iTunes vouchers or a touch-screen phone. What was she thinking?

I'm a bit concerned about her lack of ambition as well. Settling for 10p a week pocket money? Seriously? I know stuff was cheaper back then, but that's taking the mickey. What could she possibly have bought with 10p? I suppose she could have saved up for six weeks and treated herself to a Mars bar – she really loves them!

I've never actually heard of the bands she's written down, but that isn't particularly surprising cos I haven't heard of any of the music that she listens to now either. It's always really embarrassing whenever she takes me and Alice anywhere in the car. She goes on about developing our musical education and then puts on a load of rubbish that nobody would ever want to listen to.

I return the book to the box and slide the whole thing into my wardrobe, pushing it to the back. It's just as I thought – funny, but irrelevant to me in every way.

I'm just finishing my maths homework when Mum calls me down for tea. I've been repeating this maths homework now for the best part of two and a half weeks and every time I hand it in Mrs Woods hands it straight back with a 'Not good enough, Olivia'. I have literally no idea what I need to do to improve it, so today I have resorted to the only option available to me. The homework is to do with some magic cube (nothing remotely magical about it as far as I can see) and I have taken the drastic action of drawing all the cubes again and colouring them in with the nicest felt tips that I could find – had to search in my old art box for ages to find any that hadn't run out. If she isn't happy with it tomorrow, then I can do nothing more. I have utilized every mathematical and non-mathematical skill that I have and I am now empty of ideas – so this had better work . . .

I walk into the kitchen and instantly stub my toe on the big cardboard box that is, for no reason whatsoever, sitting in the middle of the floor.

'Isaac Ellis!' I roar, hopping around the kitchen in agony and clutching my foot.

'What?' asks Isaac, who is sitting at the table. He takes one earphone out of his ear. Evidently I am not important enough today to have his full attention.

'Do you think it is remotely possible that you

could *not* constantly leave this stinking pile of old junk in the doorway?'

'Yes, it is possible that I don't leave it there constantly. Yesterday I left it in the bathroom,' he says, turning away from me. This conversation is boring him.

'Yes, well, maybe, if I find it in my way again, I'll leave it outside for the bin men,' I spit. I know this is unwise, but I am fed up with the way we all have to tiptoe around Isaac and what he wants. It's so unfair – the minute I leave so much as a shoe on the floor in the hallway I'm told to tidy it up.

'Olivia,' warns Mum, casting a look at me, but I am too cross to pay attention.

'I could actually break my neck if I fell over that box of old tat.'

Isaac takes both earphones out now and turns off his iPod, very slowly. He rarely loses his temper, not since Dad taught him how to count to twenty before saying anything if someone is upsetting him. I watch him, seeing him counting in his head, and wonder what he'll do when he gets there.

Isaac's box is very precious to him. The box itself is nothing special but it is full of really important things that Isaac can't do without. He's had it forever and every now and then he'll add something to it, but he'll never take anything out. I can't see why he wants any of it. It's all old and a bit manky – stuff like a Coke can that Dad gave him when they went to watch football. (The one and only time *that* happened, Isaac totally spun out with all the crowds and they ended up sitting in the car for most of the time. I'd have thought he'd want to forget that event, personally.) There's a bit of clay that's moulded into some weird shape: I don't think even Isaac knows what it is, but apparently it's necessary for his very survival. Then there's stuff like a badge saying *Happy Second Birthday* and a totally disgusting feather that he plucked off a dead bird in the garden. Like I said, none of it makes any sense to anyone other than him. But Mum says that it doesn't hurt anyone and makes him feel secure, so we mustn't make a big deal of it.

Isaac's obviously counted to twenty because he gets up and walks over to me. I hold my breath. Isaac isn't often violent but we've had some fairly big fights in the past. This time, though, he just picks up his box.

'It's not tat,' he mutters, and goes through to the living room.

I feel awful. I know it's wrong to try to wind

him up, but he does get all the attention round here and sometimes I just can't help it. Mum sighs at me, but gives Isaac a big thumbs-up when he comes back in and sits down at the table.

'Good choice, Isaac. Well done for ignoring your sister,' she says pointedly.

Yes, all right – I feel bad enough already. It would have been easier if he'd had a meltdown. Now I just feel a bit rubbish.

Dad comes in and the rest of our meal passes as uneventfully as a meal in the Ellis family can do. There is a moment of crisis when Isaac's tomato ketchup oozes perilously close to his peas – he cannot stand bits of his food touching each other and has been known to leave the table in a strop if this happens. However, disaster is averted when I leap to the rescue and spoon up the excess sauce before it reaches the vegetables – and nicely land myself back in the parental good books, so a success all round.

After tea we do our jobs. Isaac checks the chart and happily informs me that it's my turn to dry up. He races through the washing-up with surprising speed – usually he has to make sure that each plate has been scrubbed thirty-five times or something, and then dashes into the living room to put the TV on. It takes me ages to finish the drying but I don't mind because I'm still feeling pretty guilty about being unkind to Isaac.

I finally finish and walk into the living room where I stop dead in the middle of the floor. I can't believe it! There, on *my* side of the sofa, where I always sit to watch television, is Isaac's box. His grubby, smelly box, that I demanded he move, is sitting in pride of place and resting on my favourite, comfy cushion. And Isaac is sitting upright next to it, watching excitedly for my reaction.

'What? Not OK! Mum, Dad – *tell him*!' I squeal.

Isaac bursts out laughing and Mum and Dad join in. I stand with my hands on my hips for a few more seconds and then start giggling. I walk over to Isaac and give him a high-five before settling down on the floor, which is where I spend the rest of the evening. Every now and again, one of us will look over at the box and start sniggering again. In the ad break I fetch my camera and take a picture of Dad pointing at the box and laughing. That can be 'amused'.

It's the best evening we've had in ages and all because of my brother. You see, Isaac doesn't do joking. With Isaac, it either 'is' or it 'isn't', and jokes are based on 'what-ifs' and 'maybes'. He was mad at me, but while he counted to twenty he thought of a way to get me back that was *funny*. It might not be the best joke you've ever heard, but in my family it's the most hilarious thing we've ever seen Isaac do.

That makes today a pretty good day. I'm starting to think I might have got it wrong about Mum and Dad too – surely two people who laugh like that together can't have fallen out of love?

Seven Weeks Before

I'm in a bad mood. Things are getting really weird around here, and that's saying something for Family Weirdness from Weirdsville. Mum and Dad aren't arguing any more, but Mum is constantly exhausted and Dad looks really stressed out. I came in from school the other day and he was in the hall, talking to someone on the phone. He sounded upset and when he saw me he looked really guilty and said goodbye and hung up quickly. I asked him who he was talking to and he said it was Aunt Leah – so why did he look worried when he saw me? On the upside, there've been loads of chances to take photos of different emotions – I've got 'tired' and 'cross' and 'frustrated', and yesterday I got 'worried'. Nobody has shown 'excited', though, so I had to set my camera up with a timer and act that one out myself.

Mum and Dad are out now – I'm not sure where – and Isaac is, as usual, in his room. I am super-bored. There's nothing to do around here and Alice has gone away with her dad for the weekend. Earlier I printed all my photos and pinned them up in a row on the kitchen wall, next to the huge wall planner that shows every detail of our family's life. I made a label for each photo so that Isaac can tell at a glance how we are all feeling. Those drawings that he used to have were rubbish; I'm not surprised that they didn't teach him anything. Mum found them for me when I told her exactly what my idea was, and I know that I have *never* seen anyone with a face like some of those faces. Honestly, the guy who is supposed to look 'confused' has a mouth that is physically impossible – a mad, wavy line that looks utterly painful.

Now I'm wandering around the garden, wondering whether to tidy it up. Mum is usually out here all the time, but it doesn't look as if she's done much gardening lately. I'm not actually sure what I should do, though, and after a bit I start to feel cold – seriously, it is supposed to be spring but the temperature is arctic today. I head inside and remember the box of diaries that Mum gave

me. Might as well have another look, I think –
nothing better to do.

I grab the box out from my wardrobe and
plonk myself down on the window sill. The first
entry I read is from 1986 so Mum must have been
twelve, just a few months older than me.

26 December 1986

Everyone's downstairs and I'm sitting up here on my
bed, listening to my new personal stereo. So fab!
Didn't think Mum was going to get it for me
because she's spent months going on about how
listening to music through headphones means you
can't be involved in family conversation (she
obviously hasn't got a clue and fails to understand
that THAT'S THE WHOLE POINT!).

Finally starting to get over Smokey dying. He
was the best guinea pig in the whole wide world
but I know he's happy in heaven now. I never want
another guinea pig though - nobody can replace
Smokey in my heart.

Going to watch Ghostbusters in a bit. Ha - Leah
isn't allowed to watch it cos Mum says she's too
young and it might give her nightmares. Ha ha ha!

Had a brilliant Xmas. Here's my list of what I got:

Father Christmas - cool top, cool tights, Bon Jovi tape, bubble bath, selection box, apple, orange and a new shiny 2p

Mum - personal stereo

Leah - notelets

Uncle Tony - £5 (cool!)

Grandma - torch and this diary

Uncle Andrew - Maltesers, Save the Whale T-shirt

Aunty Helen - Save the Trees poster

Quite a list, hey!

I'm going to write every day about everything that happens to me and share all my secrets with you. What do you think about boyfriends? I don't know. I wish that boys (nice ones) liked me. I think I'd like to have a real boyfriend - not to kiss, just someone who would like me and play Monopoly with me (Mum hates it and Leah moans if she loses).

See you tomorrow!

Rachel

xxxxxxxxxxxxxx

Oh, my actual goodness! My mum was a bit mental when she was my age. Wanting a boyfriend to play *Monopoly* with? Seriously? What's wrong with wanting to be kissed? Actually, I wonder how old she was when she had her first kiss – must remember to ask her!

Quite funny reading about Aunt Leah, though. She's really funky (sometimes I wish that she was my mum instead – she hasn't got any kids and when we go to stay with her we always do really cool things). Can't imagine her being too little to watch *Ghostbusters*. I must have seen that when I was about eight at Alice's house when we had a sleepover, and her dad forgot we were still awake so we stayed up until 2 a.m. watching old films on TV! Don't think I mentioned it to Mum at the time, though ... And Leah would *never* give Mum anything as naff as notelets for a present now – on her last birthday she gave her an amazing sarong that she'd brought back from somewhere exotic and a voucher for a spa day.

Mum's list of Christmas presents is a bit stingy. Last year, I got my new iPod, a make-your-own perfume set, about a million books, a boom box for my iPod, £80, and loads more stuff that I can't even remember now. Mum seems over the moon with £5 – but I suppose this *is* the person who dreamt of 10p a week pocket money, so £5 must have made her feel like a millionaire.

I turn the page and read the next entry.

4th January 1987
Dear Diary,
It is 1987! Mum woke me up at ten to twelve and we went outside to see the New Year in. This morning she made me go out of the back door and run round the house to the front door with a piece of coal. Not sure what that was all about, to be honest - something to do with me having to be the first person to come into the house in the New Year because I've got the darkest hair in our family. Sounds like a load of old cobblers to me, but it made her happy so I went along with it. Honestly, when I'm a grown-up I am NEVER going to make my kids do stupid things like that!

Last night I cried for Smokey and nobody knew. It was really sad, just lying in the dark and sobbing on my own. If I do ever get a new guinea pig I will call it Blackberry. Or maybe Mungo.

I check the date of the diary again, just to make sure I've got it right. But yes, sadly, my mother really *was* almost the same age as me when she wrote this. In fact, she was actually a little bit older than I am. I get that she was sad about the guinea pig dying, but she certainly seems to be going on about it a bit. She's always saying that kids grow up faster these days. I think that must be true, cos there's no way that I'd write something like this in my diary. If I had one. Which I don't, cos I don't trust Mum not to read it and then go totally ballistic when she reads something she doesn't like. Anyway, who has time to write a diary these days?

Had to wash my hair ready for school tomorrow - yuck! Hate doing it cos Mum INSISTS that I have to rinse it until every bit squeaks and we've always run out of hot water well before that happens. Please let somebody ask me out this year. This year I'm gonna be thirteen! Definitely old enough for a boyfriend, surely?

I'm gonna work really hard this year to make Mum proud of me. I've decided to write some rules for myself - here they are:

1. Be nice and friendly to family, especially Leah.
2. Work harder at school, particularly in stupid maths.
3. Pass grade 3 on flute.
4. Eat more (and not whinge at Mum's cooking, even when it IS gross).
5. NOT get spots.
6. Have more baths.
7. Try to not be sad about Smokey.
8. Try to love another guinea pig.
9. Get a boyfriend - if I don't get one this year then I never will.

Hey, it'll be a miracle if I can do all that in ONE year!

Bye

Rachel

XXXXXXXXXXXXXXXXX

OK, this is a bit more interesting! If I ignore the fact that my teenage mother seems to be equally obsessed with guinea pigs as she is with boys, then I suppose some of what she's written makes sense to me. I definitely know how she feels about wanting a boyfriend, that's for sure. Everyone else

in my year at school has had at least one boyfriend –
even Alice went out with dopey Pete for about
two hours at the school disco. Nothing actually
happened and they didn't even really speak to each
other, but at least everyone knows that someone
fancied her.

Maybe I'm a late developer and I've inherited it
from Mum. She's already confessed that she passed
her rubbishness at maths on to me so that'd be
about right. Now I'll have to keep on reading her
diaries to see how she solved the problem –
perhaps she's right and there *are* some good rules
in here. Maybe I'll get some top tips for how to
let Ben know I'm interested in him.

I am loving her list of rules – she was obviously
obsessed with rules even back then! Got to admire
her confidence. I too would like not to get spots
and to find a boyfriend. Who knew that you just
had to make it a life rule! Number 4 is a bit ironic,
though. I used to love Granny's cooking – it was
definitely an improvement on Mum's, that's for
sure. Actually, it feels a bit weird seeing Mum
write about Granny. She died when I was nine and
it was so sad that I tried for ages not to really
think about her – and I suppose I kind of got into
the habit of forgetting, so that I didn't feel unhappy.

I'm wondering whether to delve further when I hear the front door slam. A few moments later I hear the sound of Mum coming upstairs. I get ready to brandish the diary at her and make her laugh by reminding her of her long-lost love for Smokey the guinea pig and her obvious reluctance to keep clean (and to accuse her of hypocrisy – she always asks me if I've rinsed my hair until it squeaks and every New Year's Day, even if it's pouring with rain or freezing cold, she makes me do that coal thing and she still doesn't know what it's supposed to mean cos I've asked her). She doesn't come into my room, though, and instead I hear her go into her bedroom and close the door.

Dad calls Isaac and me down not long after and, once I've navigated Isaac's box (keeping my mouth firmly shut this time), we sit down at the table.

'Where's Mum?' I ask. Dad puts a pan of pasta down and goes back to the stove to dish up the sauce into a separate bowl.

'She's really tired today, Liv – she's gone to bed,' he says, with his back to me.

'No!' says Isaac. 'We all eat as a family – that's the rule!'

'Not today, mate,' says Dad. 'Mum needs to rest.'

Isaac slams his fork down on to the table. I cringe, knowing what's coming.

'You *don't* break a rule!' he shouts at Dad. 'I'm here, Liv's here, you're here – and Mum should be here. That's what we agreed and that's the rule.'

Dad sighs. 'I'm sorry, Isaac, but sometimes we can't always keep all the rules. Things change and we have to be flexible.'

I can see, and so can Dad, that Isaac is not listening to him. Some of the rules in our house are there to help Isaac make sense of everything and some are there to help him understand how to behave. The rule about everyone sitting down at the table before we can start eating happened because Isaac used to go into the kitchen any time he felt like it and eat all the food that he could find. Mum and Dad kept going to cook our meals and finding that half the ingredients were missing. For a boy who has such strong opinions on so many things, he's surprisingly not fussy about what he'll eat – I've seen him eating whole blocks of butter or all the cheese in the fridge like I would eat a biscuit or an apple.

So this rule was made, and once Isaac understands a rule there is no changing it unless he can be persuaded that it has been turned into a new rule. And that doesn't happen overnight.

Dad sits down and passes me the pasta. 'Here you are, Liv, help yourself,' he says.

I serve myself and then reach over for the sauce. 'Yummy – thanks, Dad!' I say, hoping that Isaac doesn't make a huge scene.

'Come on, Isaac, tuck in!' says Dad cheerily, handing Isaac a big plate with pasta on one side and sauce very firmly on the other side, like two armies lining up for battle.

Dad and I eat our meal, but Isaac just sits there, hands on the table and staring at his food. I hear his tummy rumble.

'It sounds like you're starving – just eat a little bit of it. It's really good,' I say.

'Can't eat,' he mutters, refusing to look up. 'Mustn't eat until everyone is sitting at the table.'

I look at Dad in despair.

'Can't Mum just come and sit with us for a bit?' I ask him. I'm suddenly feeling worried. Mum knows how important the rules are, and if any of us are ever ill we still try really hard to keep everything normal for Isaac. It's not always easy, but it's better than the meltdowns that happen if things are different.

Dad suddenly looks cross – but I don't think he's mad at me.

'Isaac is just going to have to learn to cope with change,' he says, so quietly I can barely hear him. 'Just let him be, Liv. He'll eat if he's hungry.'

I am in total shock. Dad knows, as much as anyone else, that Isaac will *not* eat just because he's hungry. If something upsets him, then he either has a huge tantrum or goes really quiet and won't do anything. That's why we have the rules – to keep him safe and to keep a routine.

Something is really, really wrong and I'm scared for Isaac and I'm scared for me.

Six Weeks
Before

I am sitting with Isaac watching television, glad to be home after the world's worst day at school (Moronic Louise told Ben that I'd been saying nasty things about him. I don't know if he believed her but it's made me feel kind of awkward around him), when Dad tells us that he wants us to go upstairs. I start to get up, but he stops me.

'Not yet, Liv,' he says. 'Mum and I want to talk to you about something important. Just wait here until I call you – it'll be a few minutes.' He leaves the room and I hear him go upstairs. Isaac changes the TV channel and I sit wondering what they might be about to tell us. The clue must be in Dad's voice. If he sounded sad, then I reckon I was right all along and they're getting a divorce. If he sounded happy, then maybe they're planning to give us a treat? I look out of the window, replaying

Dad's voice in my head. The garden is looking even more of a state at the moment. Mum is the only person who actually enjoys gardening and since she's been ill everything looks as if it's been growing at double speed. I'm thinking really hard but it's impossible to work out how Dad sounded – it's like he's got a whole new emotion that I haven't a name for.

Isaac has flicked TV channels again and suddenly my favourite advert for Disneyland is on the screen. And it gets me thinking. Maybe that's what they want to talk to us about? After all, I've dropped enough hints about it that they'd have to be stupid not to notice. I've even looked up loads of Walt Disney quotes on the Internet and started leaving them on Post-it notes on the fridge door. I thought that if I could convince them it might be educational, then they might start to think it was a good idea. My absolute favourite quote is Walt Disney saying that if you can dream it, then you can do it. Well, I have been dreaming about going to Disneyland forever, so maybe, finally, I will get to live my dream!

Isaac suddenly changes channels again, but my advert isn't finished so I'm struggling to grab the remote off him, when I hear Dad calling us. His voice sounds a bit funny and I start to feel excited. Something big is happening, that's for sure!

He and Mum are in their bedroom. Mum hasn't got out of bed for a few days. I've been rushing in there to say goodbye before school and going in to say goodnight at bedtime, but I've been really busy with homework and seeing Alice, and she's usually asleep when I do go in. Anyway, I'm guessing she's got that horrible flu that everyone is going on about and I *really* don't want to catch it. I'm ninety-nine per cent sure that Moronic Louise fancies Ben and would totally make the most of me being away from school to tell him awful things about me and to make her move.

It seems a bit weird to be all going in there together and I suddenly feel a bit shy. I stand in the doorway, unsure whether I should go in or not.

'Come and sit here with me,' calls Mum, patting the side of her bed. She is sitting up and wearing a new pair of pyjamas – in fact, she looks better than she's looked all week. I run over and cuddle up to her. I won't admit it but I've really missed her since she got ill. I've been reading her diary a bit more but it's not the same as talking to her properly. Isaac sits next to Dad at the bottom of the bed and I wonder again what they're going to tell us.

Actually, I'm pretty certain that I guessed it right downstairs. I reckon that it'd be the perfect time to whisk us all away on holiday. Mum's been really tired and poorly for ages now, so she's got to get better soon. It'd probably really help her to have a break. And possibly – I can hardly bear to think about it – almost definitely, it's the place that I've *always* wanted to go! That'd explain why they wanted to make a big deal out of telling us, and why Dad said 'Wait and see what happens' when I was going on about it again a few weeks ago. Oh my goodness, Alice is going to be *so* jealous.

Dad asks Isaac to take his earphones out for a moment and I can hardly sit still I'm so excited.

'We wanted you both in here together so that we can tell you something,' starts Dad. His voice sounds even weirder than it did downstairs. 'It's a really big thing that we need to talk about and –'

'I *knew* it!' I squeal, unable to keep quiet any longer. 'You are the *best* parents *ever*!'

'Liv,' says Dad. 'Just listen for a minute.'

But I have dreamt of this moment for so long

that nothing can stop me. I leap to my feet. 'Thank you, thank you, thank you! When are we going? Oh – I cannot *wait* to tell Alice! It'll be the best holiday in the world!'

'Going where?' asks Isaac, looking confused.

'Oh, Isaac, you'll love it. Seriously. I'll show you everything on the website so you know what to expect – they've got the biggest rides, loads of shows – oh, it's gonna be epic!'

'*LIV!*' shouts Dad suddenly, in an awful kind of voice. I look at him. His face is red and he looks like he's about to blow up or something. 'Will you be quiet for one minute and *listen*!'

Mum takes hold of my arm. 'Liv – I don't know what you think we're going to say, but we're not talking about holidays.'

I flop down on the bed, feeling utterly deflated. Just for a moment there, I thought that my terminally uncool parents were actually going to do something funky. I mean, I've wanted to go to Disneyland since I was about three, and it's not as if I haven't gone on about it enough. Everyone knows it's my life's ambition. Life is *so* unfair.

I'm barely even listening now to what Mum is saying; I'm too busy fighting back the tears of frustration. I can hear that she's speaking but for some reason, my head can't make sense of the words coming out of her mouth.

'Liv? Did you hear any of what I just said?' Mum asks gently. Dad is standing now, and pacing up and down the room, muttering under his breath that it is too hard and he isn't ready for this.

I think about the words that I just heard Mum utter and a cold chill suddenly washes over me. I look at her quickly, confused – *what* did she just say?

She's quiet now, waiting for my reaction. I don't know what to say. I can't even think properly. All that's going through my mind is that nobody has made our packed lunches for tomorrow and Dad always puts the wrong spread in Isaac's sandwiches, so I'd better do it. That Isaac is going to have to learn an awful lot of new rules. That I really, really wish the worst thing that could have happened to my family was my parents getting a divorce, because that would have been a million times better than this. And that I have no idea where the tears streaming down my face are coming from because inside I feel cold and empty.

Mum has pulled me into her arms and is rubbing the small of my back – and that just makes me cry even more because who is going to do that for Isaac when she's gone? I don't even like having my back rubbed, but I don't move because I think it might be making her feel better and I don't want to be anywhere but here.

We sit like that for ages and eventually I need to blow my nose, and I don't want to wreck Mum's new pyjamas so I pull myself up. Isaac is sitting at the end of the bed, with Dad next to him. He's put his earphones back in and is engrossed in his music, and I wonder if he even understands that our whole world has just caved in.

Mum looks over at Dad and tries to smile but fails. 'A cup of tea would be really good right now,' she says, with a sob in her voice.

I get up and Dad comes over to Mum. He sits down and pulls her to him, stroking her hair and murmuring words that I can't hear. I feel like we shouldn't be here, so I take Isaac's hand and say that we'll go and put the kettle on. As we reach the door, Isaac suddenly stops and turns round.

'So where are we actually going then? Cos I need lots of time to get ready, remember, and you need to get me an information book so I know what to expect and what the rules are.'

I pull him out of the room, thinking that I have no idea how much time we have to get ready and that I'm not actually sure there even *is* an information book to help us with this. But I really wish there was because I could definitely do with some rules right now.

Five Weeks
Before

The funny thing about being utterly terrified and scared and miserable is that it isn't consistent. I'm not saying that any of us feel better about what's going on with Mum, but the awfulness of the first twenty-four hours just couldn't carry on all day, every day. Mum has actually been up and out of bed this week, and while I wouldn't say that things are back to normal, we're kind of finding a new 'normal'. The first night after she told us, I couldn't sleep at all – every time I closed my eyes it felt like a nightmare and in the end, I got up and opened her diary.

18 April 1987
It's Easter Day tomorrow! I'm hoping for loads of Easter eggs. I still miss Smokey and I haven't got a boyfriend. Nobody likes me. All the boys think I'm a

big mouth. I really like Michael who sits behind me in maths but all he does is hit me. Mum says that's how twelve-year-old boys show they like you but I think she doesn't know WHAT she's talking about. Seriously - every time he sees me he just whacks me with his pencil case, says something rude about how I look and runs off with his mates, and I REALLY like him - it's SO embarrassing!

Must go - time to watch telly.

Rachel
xxx

That could be me writing that! That's exactly what Ben has started doing – I've actually got a bruise on my arm from where he threw a football at me. Can't believe it means he likes me, though. I'm with Mum – Granny must have been a bit bonkers when she said that.

29 April 1987
I'm SO excited! I'm going to France on the school trip on Monday - it's the first time I've ever been abroad! I can't wait. But I am a bit worried about leaving Mum and Leah on their own. I always check

that the back door is locked and the electricity is turned off at all the sockets before I go to bed - hope Mum remembers to do it when I'm not here.

The next entry is for a month later. There's nothing about how her school trip went. She's not very good at writing regularly. I wonder what made her think that the things she *did* write about were so important?

27 May 1987

Stop the clocks! Hold the phones! Today is a momentous day that will go down in history. Patrick told Beth that Jason told him that Michael said that he fancies me! Hurray! I am no longer the unlovable Rachel, only girl in the universe who nobody finds attractive. It is so excellent!

I've actually decided that I don't like Michael any more. But that's not the point, is it? So happy today - I will NEVER forget this day as long as I live . . .!

I am actually in love with four and a half boys. I really like Matt but he's a bit of a goody-goody. Gary is a creep but I like him too, and actually I'd just settle for him liking me. Simon is quite nice but would never notice someone like me. Michael is a laugh but too short. Chris is the substitute. It's not funny really - how would you like it if you couldn't even look at a boy without falling in love with him?

Yesterday was school fund-raising day for our local hospital. Beth and I raised £33.42 by going around all day with our legs tied together. And I mean ALL DAY! Even when we went to the loo! It was hilarious.

Reading this made me laugh, but then I remembered about Mum and that everything is not OK, and I felt really bad for laughing. I ended up creeping into Mum and Dad's room later that night. Dad was asleep, but Mum was awake so I lay down next to her and we whispered for hours. I told her about what I'd read in her diary and she laughed and said that, when she was my age, she thought she'd *never* get a boyfriend. She said that Granny always used to tell her that her time would come and that right now, she was so clever and beautiful that she intimidated boys – but that one day they'd get brave and it'd all change.

That made me smile because she's always saying that to me too.

Then Mum put her arm round me and told me

to close my eyes and she sang me a lullaby – the tune I'd heard her humming the other day, which seems like a lifetime ago now – and I remembered how she always used to sing it to me if I was having trouble sleeping.

> *'Lay thee down now and rest,*
> *May thy slumber be blessed.'*

Mum sang quietly, and as I drifted off to sleep I thought about the words and thought that it was the most beautiful song that I had ever heard.

Now, though, with Mum making our lunches and being there when we come home from school, it feels as if all that was a nasty dream that we can start to move on from.

Dad has been introducing some new rules to the house. The first one is that we can eat our meals when everyone who *intends to eat* is sitting down. It's clever, what he's done there. It's virtually the same rule as before, but by changing it just a bit, mealtimes can be more flexible yet Isaac still feels that he is keeping the rule.

Tonight, I am sitting on the stairs waiting for the timer to buzz so that I can get into the bathroom.

If left to his own devices, Isaac will sit in the bath for *hours*. The water will be cold and the rest of the family will be hopping up and down outside, but he won't come out. Isaac loves water. (This has given Mum and Dad quite a few scares over the years. They taught him to swim pretty quickly when they realized that if they were anywhere within three miles of water Isaac would end up wet before too long.) So Isaac has a rule that he can stay in the bath until his thirty-minute timer buzzes. He sticks to this rule rigidly and won't get out of the water one minute early – even if you're hammering on the door with your legs crossed and begging him to let you in.

I'm finding it hard to believe that Mum is really all that ill. She's been so energetic this week. On Thursday I came home from school and she was outside the front of our house, frantically weeding the flower beds. She said that they needed tidying and Dad's been saying he'll get round to it forever, so she was taking matters into her own hands. She certainly didn't seem ill to me.

I am getting really bored waiting for Isaac when Mum comes upstairs and sees me sitting there.

'Have you got time for a new rule?' she asks me.

'Oh, Mum!' I groan. 'What now? Because Dad's

already told Isaac that trying to make scrambled eggs at 4 a.m. is definitely a no-no.' Honestly, sometimes I find it amazing that my brother hasn't burnt our house to the ground with his night-time adventures.

'This isn't a rule for Isaac – it's for you!' says Mum, beckoning me to follow her and heading into her room. She's made me curious now so I follow her, but I'll be really annoyed if this is some lame attempt to get me to do a chore.

Mum is standing by her dressing table and has put out all of her make-up. She has some really nice stuff (mostly given to her by Leah, I must add) and is highly possessive about it. I've given up trying to convince her to let me use it – all I've got is a strawberry lipgloss and some fairy-dust body glitter. I mean, seriously, how old does she think I am?

Mum pulls out the stool in front of her table and guides me into it. She stands behind me and talks to me in the mirror.

'It's time you learnt the rules for how to make the most of your beautiful looks,' she informs me. '*Not* that I'm agreeing to you wearing make-up before you're sixteen,' she adds quickly as I start to grin. 'It's just something that you need to learn.

Granny taught me and I'm teaching you. Besides, you're twelve next week and that's a really great age to start looking after your skin.'

I look at all the stuff that she's laid out in front of me. Lotions and potions in loads of different-shaped bottles – and a *lot* of cotton wool.

'The first and most important thing to remember is that beautiful skin is healthy skin,' she says, and picks up a bottle marked *cleanser*. I groan inside. I thought this would be fun, like putting make-up on that freaky, disembodied plastic head that Granny brought out of the attic and said that Mum spent so much time playing with when she was a girl. Instead, Mum's making it sound like a lot of work.

'It does require a bit of effort,' says Mum, as if reading my mind. 'But the most expensive, luxurious make-up in the world cannot cover up a spotty, greasy face.'

I have to agree with her there. Moronic Louise wears make-up all the time at weekends and if you're ever unfortunate enough to bump into her in town, it can be very hard not to stare at the sight of her bright red lips fighting with her bright red pimples for attention. Not a good look.

Mum has squirted some of the cleanser on to

cotton wool and is gently but firmly wiping my face with it. It's quite relaxing actually.

'Do you ever wash your face, Liv?' asks Mum. How rude!

'Of course I do,' I reply, feeling slightly less relaxed.

'Do you wash it *properly*? Get rid of all the dirt?' questions Mum.

I'm insulted now. I thought this was meant to be a nice experience.

'Yes, Mum,' I snap. 'I am one hundred per cent confident that my face is free from any dirt. I think I'd see it, don't you? I'm not like Isaac, you know – I can actually eat without spreading half of my meal across my face!'

'OK, OK,' says Mum, holding her hands up in mock-surrender, 'if you're absolutely sure. Just take a little look at this cotton wool, though.'

She holds out the cotton wool that she's been cleaning my face with and my jaw hits the floor (or should that be my dirty, manky, filthy jaw hits the floor?). The cotton wool is *black* – well, maybe browny-grey, but disgusting-looking, all the same.

Mum bursts out laughing at my expression and throws the offending item in the bin before bending down to hug me.

'Have I got your attention now, sweetheart?' she grins, but I am too shocked to answer her and am busy scrutinizing my face in the mirror to see what else I have failed to notice.

'Don't worry, Liv – you're gorgeous,' says Mum, straightening up and squirting something else on to yet more cotton wool. 'You've got lovely skin – you can thank your dad for that – but it's always a good rule to look after what you've got. Don't take anything for granted.'

Our eyes meet in the mirror and for a moment I think I might start crying, but Mum smiles at me and starts showing me the next step in my new beauty regime.

We spend the next thirty minutes cleansing, toning and moisturizing, and then, much to my delight, Mum shows me how to apply eyeliner and eyeshadow and mascara. She even lets me put some lipstick on, but draws the line at foundation and blusher because she says it'll ruin all the good work we've done on cleaning my skin. Then, the best bit – she lets me practise on *her*! I try really hard to do a good job, but it's very difficult to keep your hand steady and I end up drawing a jerky line under her eyes that she says makes her look about twenty years older than she is.

When I'm finished, she looks in the mirror and says that I could have a great future ahead of me as a special-effects artist and then we start laughing, and we laugh so much that tears roll down our faces and then the make-up starts running and that makes us laugh even more. I'm laughing so much that my stomach hurts – in fact I can't remember laughing this hard in ages. Then, just as I'm gasping in a deep breath and feeling like I might collapse with laughter, I glance over at Mum. She's still laughing but I can see that her face, beneath my awful makeover, is scrunched up as if she's in actual, real pain and not just laughter aches.

I forgot. For one moment I actually forgot about what is happening to Mum and I laughed as if there was nothing wrong. I feel like I've just walked into a brick wall and all I can do is stand there and look at her, my head racing with thoughts that I don't want to be having.

Mum sees that I've stopped laughing and sits down on her bed, pulling me next to her. We sit for a while, cuddled up together, and when I start to get fidgety and move away, I see that some of my make-up has rubbed off on her white shirt.

'OK, Liv?' asks Mum, and I nod at her. 'It's OK

to have some fun, you know,' she tells me quietly. 'It's good to make happy memories.'

I want to tell her that I don't want memories – I want her. But I don't say a word. I think that maybe the happy memories aren't just for me – perhaps she thinks she can take them with her. And I make a silent promise to give Mum as many happy memories as I can. We sit for a little while longer and then Mum calls Dad to take a photo of us. We stand next to the door with our arms round each other and pull the most hideous faces possible – I've got my tongue out and Mum is rolling her eyes and puffing out her cheeks – and she says that when the photo is printed it should be labelled 'Beauty and the Beast'!

After that I can finally get in the bathroom cos Isaac's buzzer has gone and he's back in his room. I wash off the make-up and wish that days like today could last forever or be put in a bottle like the ones on Mum's dressing table, so I could take it out whenever I wanted.

I've been reading Mum's diaries quite a lot this week. Some of it's a bit boring (quite amazing actually, what she thought was worth writing about), but some of her entries have really made me laugh. It's kind of cool in a way, like I'm getting to meet my mum when she was young. I think we might've been friends if we were born at the same time. One thing's for sure – she is *so totally* different now she's grown-up. I've got as far as 1987, so she was nearly thirteen when she was writing this stuff, although she doesn't sound any older than me, to be honest – and I'm not even twelve until next week, which I totally don't even want to think about. The very idea of celebrating a birthday seems absolutely wrong. She's still going on about boys but at least she seems to have forgotten about the guinea pig.

After having such a great time with Mum and the make-up lesson, I'm not in the mood to go straight to bed so I decide to keep on reading from where I left off. The last thing I read was yet another list of her Christmas presents and her telling the diary her views on nudist camps – apparently they're OK if the nudists are religious. Must remember to ask her about that.

19 August 1987
At Grandma's. She's got a headache so not expecting today to be much fun. Wondering what the next year will be like at school. I really like

Michael again but we're such good friends now -
d'you think it would make everything weird if we
went out with each other? And what if we broke
up? Oh - I don't know . . .

10 November 1987
Had big argument with Mum this morning when she
saw me trying to sneak out to school wearing
eyeliner (well, she says 'sneak', I say 'walk').
Honestly, she has no idea about what it's like being
a teenager today - and I'm an ideal teenager -
loads of kids I know give their parents a much
harder time than I do. Told her that but she
refused to change her mind. So unfair.

Hmm. Think I might need to wave this particular
diary entry in front of Mum tomorrow – remind
her how she felt when her unreasonable mother
wouldn't let her do stuff that everyone else is
doing! I read a few more entries where she is
mostly going on about a war somewhere far
away – it's all pretty boring so I close the diaries,
get into bed and turn off my lamp.

Mum was certainly a bit of a worrier when she
was a teenager, although that's not surprising
because she worries about everything now too.

She's good in an emergency, though – she always manages to say something that makes you realize it's not as bad as you first thought it was.

I start to think about who will help me and Isaac when we get into trouble. Dad's great, but he isn't really into talking about how you feel. Mum's always the one who sits down with me and talks about stuff for ages and ages.

There suddenly seem much bigger things to worry about than make-up.

Four Weeks Before

It's my birthday today. I wake up feeling flat and think that I really can't be bothered – trying to pretend that we're all having a good time is going to seem totally false and I already wish it was tomorrow. I get out of bed and put on my dressing gown, hoping that nobody else is awake and I can at least eat some breakfast without having to fake being happy.

I go downstairs and open the kitchen door.

'SURPRISE!' shout Mum and Dad, leaping up from the table and rushing over to give me a huge hug. Isaac stays sitting down but grins at me nervously – being surprised is his idea of hell and he's not that keen on surprising anyone else either.

'Open your presents, Liv!' says Mum, leading me over to my seat where there is a big pile of brightly wrapped gifts waiting.

Dad laughs. 'Give the girl a chance to sit down, Rachel! Cup of tea and a bacon butty, Liv?'

I nod at him in relief. Tea and a bacon butty is our family's traditional birthday breakfast – it's good to see that some things have stayed the same. Mum, on the other hand, is doing my head in. She normally makes us open our presents slowly, partly so we 'show appreciation of the effort that people have gone to' and partly so that we don't rip the wrapping paper which she will hoard in a drawer, and which I have never, to this day, seen her re-use.

Today, though, she is urging me to dive into the presents with wild abandon. Last year this would have made me feel pleased, but now it dawns on me that maybe she thinks she won't get to see me do this again. Now I'm the one who wants to open the presents slowly. Maybe if I make present-opening last forever, then she'll never leave me.

'Here you go, beautiful birthday girl,' says Dad, putting a hot mug down in front of me. He ruffles my hair and I know that he understands how much today sucks.

Mum thrusts a beautifully wrapped box at me.

'Open this one first – it's from Isaac.' I undo the

ribbon and gasp – inside is the most gorgeous, delicate necklace I've ever seen. It's got a thin, silver chain and a tiny, daisy-shaped flower on the end. Embedded in the flower are four sparkling, silver gems – one for each of us, I think to myself.

'Isaac, it's amazing! You really shouldn't have!' I exclaim, glancing over at Dad and smiling. He smiles back – of course Isaac didn't choose this, but Dad would never tell!

I get up and give Isaac a thank-you pat on the arm. Then I ask Dad to fasten the chain round my neck and I glance at myself in the mirror above the mantelpiece.

'It's perfect – I love it,' I say.

I sit back down. Mum is busying herself with buttering some toast and I can tell that she's struggling not to cry. I try to distract her. 'Which one shall I open next, Mum?' I ask her.

'This one,' she says, passing me a box. 'It's from me and Dad, but Dad's done all the work choosing it.'

I give it a shake. 'Careful, Liv!' Dad says quickly. 'Might want to be a bit gentle with this one.' I look at him. His eyes are shining and he is watching me intently. I haven't seen him this interested in present-opening since – well, ever. Whatever is inside this wrapping paper, my dad is really excited about.

I carefully peel back the sticking tape and pull at the paper. Crikey, it's well wrapped. I reckon Dad was in charge of wrapping up as well as choosing. Mum tends to be a bit more frugal with her wrapping technique, but it looks as if he's used the whole roll of paper. I start to laugh as I pull back layer after layer, and Mum joins in. Dad is grinning but he has no idea why we're laughing! And then – I'm in. And it was worth the effort.

'Wow!' I breathe, looking at my new present in amazement. 'Really? Is it actually for me? A proper camera?'

'Who else?' laughs Mum.

I turn to Dad. 'But I thought you said not until I was a bit older?'

'You're ready, Liv,' he says simply.

'And you'll show me how to use it properly?' I ask.

'Try stopping me! I've been itching to get my hands on it since we bought it!'

'Dan!' warns Mum, rolling her eyes at me.

'I know, don't worry – I won't take over! It's

Liv's. But I can't say I won't enjoy showing her how to get the best results with it.'

And now it's my turn to feel tears welling up in my eyes. I put the box gently down on the table, as carefully as if it contained the crown jewels, and go round to where Mum and Dad are sitting. I cuddle Mum for a moment and then Dad scoops me up into a huge bear hug.

'Thank you, thank you,' I whisper to him.

'Happy birthday, Olivia. You really deserve this,' he whispers back.

The rest of breakfast time passes in a bit of a blur. I open my other gifts and they're all fab – money from lots of people and a book that I really wanted from Mum's friend, Beth. Mum tells me that Leah's present will be arriving 'at some point' – I know that Leah is really disorganized but that her present will definitely be worth waiting for.

Finally, the breakfast things are cleared away and I think it's safe enough to get my camera out of the box. Mum is worn out from all the excitement so she goes back to bed, and Isaac, having coped very well with a different start to his day, runs upstairs to the safety and normality of his pigsty of a bedroom.

Dad and I clean the table in silence and then look at each other.

'OK, I'm ready,' I say. 'I'm going in!' I open up the box and can't resist another gasp – it is the most beautiful thing I've ever owned. There, nestled on elaborate packaging, is a proper, grown-up camera – the sort of camera that I've watched my dad use for his photography for years, and the camera that I've wanted ever since I started to take my own pictures.

'I think we can agree you've done your apprenticeship, Liv – you're definitely ready for the real deal,' Dad says as I lift it out of the box.

I have always been fascinated by Dad's photographs and started wanting to take my own when I was small. To begin with, Dad let me use an old Polaroid camera that he had cluttering up his studio – it really appealed to me because I could be holding the picture in my chubby little hand only a few minutes after I'd taken it. The photos always faded, though, so next I was given a basic digital camera for Christmas when I was eight. I really loved that camera and I won a few competitions at school and one at the library in town. What I've wanted for ages, though, is a serious camera. Not something that anybody could just point and shoot, but something that demands real skill. Because this is when I feel happiest – when I'm deciding what to take a picture of and how I want it to look.

I've spent hours and hours with Dad, watching him work. He takes photographs of normal, everyday things, but in such a way that they aren't instantly recognizable. He always tells me that the most important thing to think about, when taking a picture, is the 'why'.

'*Why* do you want to photograph this today? That's what you have to ask yourself, Liv,' he'll say to me as he prowls round his subject, looking for the angle that he wants to take. 'What are you trying to say with this picture? Is it just for fun (and that's fine, by the way) or are you trying to get a message across? Maybe you're asking a question. It doesn't matter, as long as you know why you're doing it.'

Dad has never minded me following him around and has even given me my own corner in his studio, where I can work on my pictures. What he has refused to budge on is getting a decent camera for me.

'Why now?' I ask him, holding the camera in my hands and turning it over and over, inspecting every little detail.

'You've shown us how mature you are over the

last few weeks,' he answers. 'The way you're dealing with everything and helping Isaac too – we're really proud of you.'

'Thanks, Dad. I promise I'll be careful with it,' I say.

'You'd better!' he mock-growls. 'You're ready to start developing your own style now, Liv – this is not a camera that will be happy taking photographs of *Autumn Days* or *Summer Fun* or any other ludicrous theme that your school can dream up. This is the real deal. Now get out there and start shooting.'

'I thought you were going to show me how to use it?' I say.

'Yes – I am. But the best way to do that is if you have a go on your own. Explore with it, play around. You know enough not to do any damage. Bring me the results and then we'll talk about how you can get the most out of it.'

'Deal!' I say. This is perfect. I think my dad is great but I'm teeming with ideas for photos that I want to take and I don't need him holding me back. I just want to get on with it.

I grab my rucksack and chuck a couple of apples, a bottle of water and a packet of biscuits in. Dad hands me my waterproof jacket and although I grimace at him, I shove that in too. Then, camera looped carefully round my neck, I yell goodbye to Mum and head out into the great outdoors, the whole world ready for me to take award-winning photographs.

Four hours later and I'm sitting, despondent, in Dad's studio at the bottom of our garden. I'm freezing cold and drenched to the bone – my rubbish coat was no match for the downpour that happened an hour ago. The products of today's efforts are spread out on the desk in front of me. And frankly, they're a waste of printer ink.

The door creaks open and Dad comes in. I sense him standing behind me, looking over my shoulder at my pictures.

'Don't say it. I know they're awful,' I mutter.

He laughs. 'They're not awful, Liv – there's no such thing! Just a work in progress, that's what I always try to tell myself when I'm not happy with a day's work.'

'Dad! Seriously? These can, in no way, be classed as a "work in progress". I thought I was ready for this but obviously I was wrong.'

Dad spins me round on my chair and looks squarely into my eyes.

'Stop that now, young lady! This is what today was all about. You need to feel your way, develop a working relationship with the camera. It is, I agree, an amazing machine but it's only a tool. I probably take a hundred dodgy pictures before I get the right one – you know that.'

'Yes, but you know what you want to take pictures of and you have a style that's all your own. Look at my photos and tell me that they're different and interesting!'

We stare at the photographs I've taken today. There's one where I tried to show the raindrops racing down the bus shelter – but it's all blurry. There's another one of a brick wall with a flower growing out of it – way too tacky! In desperation, I have taken a few of our cat, but even she thought I was rubbish and wandered off halfway through. There are pictures of umbrellas and shop signs and a little old woman laden down with her shopping.

'They're not bad pictures, Liv,' says Dad. 'But you know what I'm going to say, don't you?'

'Yeah,' I scowl. 'Why did I take these pictures? I just wanted to be impressive. I wanted to do something different from everyone else, but all I've ended up with is a load of old rubbish.'

'And that, my precious girl, is the answer! Well

done, young Jedi knight – you have learnt the first lesson!'

'What d'you mean? I don't know what you're talking about! I haven't learnt *anything* today – that's why I'm miserable.'

'You'll take much better photos when you stop and listen to what *you* want to do. When you take a chance and let opportunity in. Not when your motivation is to be clever or to be different. You *are* different, Liv – you are unique and wonderful and one-of-a-kind. Let that part of you lead the way. I promise you, you'll be pleasantly surprised!'

I think about what Dad has said. It's true, I did spend most of today trying to be clever. I thought about that more than I actually looked at what was around me.

'But enough now – your mother has baked you a cake and it is part of your ritual birthday torture that you will have to eat it!'

'Dad!' I exclaim, but I can't help agreeing with him. Mum has a tendency to try out new and bizarre recipes for our birthday cakes. Last year I had broccoli cake – she'd seen a recipe for courgette cake but had a glut of broccoli and decided that it probably wouldn't matter if she substituted one green vegetable for another. Turns out, it really *did* matter. The cake was utterly disgusting and Isaac whispered to me that it tasted like farts. We all ate it, though – nobody wanted to let Mum know how foul it really was.

We sprint up the garden path, trying to avoid the huge hailstones that are throwing themselves from the heavens. I think that the best thing about today is that it's nearly over. It seems utterly wrong that real-life things like birthdays and parents' evening and doing the shopping should still be taking place when our world is in free fall. I hate it most when something distracts me and I forget, for just a second – the moment of remembering makes me feel sick and guilty and lost, all at the same time.

Three Weeks Before

I am so mad with Alice that I can hardly think straight. She's supposed to be my friend and friends are supposed to be kind and considerate – and neither of those words applies to her right now.

Today starts badly. My alarm clock has broken so I oversleep this morning and that means I'm late leaving the house. When I get to our corner Alice isn't there, which I think is a bit weird because we *always* wait for each other, but I know that if I don't run I'll be late for registration, so I have to go. I think that maybe she's ill and hasn't remembered to phone me, or something.

I make it into my tutor group by the skin of my teeth. Alice is in a different tutor group from me and she's not in my PE class either, so I still don't know if she is even in school by the time I get into the changing room. Sadly for me, Moronic Louise and her cronies are in my PE class, and I can see them looking over at me and sniggering while we are all getting changed.

Just as I am tying up the laces on my trainers, they swagger over. I know something is wrong the minute Louise opens her mouth. She's trying really hard to sound all casual and innocent, and failing miserably.

'Hi, Liv, how're you doing?' she trills. I grunt a response – I don't feel in the mood to waste any proper words on her. Louise is a real faker. I honestly think it has been so long since she last did anything true or genuine that she's forgotten how. Alice and I go to extreme lengths to avoid her – she's poisonous and likes to surround herself with equally toxic, although weaker, friends.

'Great news about Alice, isn't it?' she chimes in the girly, high-pitched voice that I happen to know is nothing like her actual voice.

I look up at her, wary now. 'What are you talking about?'

'You mean you don't know?' shrieks Louise, turning towards her little witches' coven and grinning manically at them. 'Girls, we have to share the excitement with Liv, don't you agree?'

There is a general giggling and nudging of each other among them.

'I have no idea what you're wittering on about, Louise, and I'm fairly certain that I'm not interested either, so if you'll get out of my way I have an appointment with a badminton racquet.' I stand up but before I can move, Louise puts her hand out.

'You'll want to hear this, trust me. I actually can't believe that she hasn't told you herself unless – oh, that must be it! She's worried about how you'll react. Poor Alice, torn between a boy and her best friend.'

'It's *so* sad,' squawks Molly. She's harmless but massively irritating. I've really had enough and I'm starting to feel worried. Alice and I don't keep secrets from each other and there's no way that she would tell Moronic Louise something before she told me – that literally could not happen. The only thing is, Louise can hardly keep still she's so excited. Whatever she thinks she knows, it's pretty big.

'You're talking a load of pants, moron,' I tell her and push past. She lets me go and then, just as I reach the changing-room door, fires her weapon.

'Of course, Alice has got no reason to worry, has she? It's not as if you even liked Ben, is it? Wouldn't go out with him if he was the last boy on earth, didn't you say?' She collapses into a heap of giggles and I leave the changing room with the sound of their laughter following me down the hall.

I'm really angry – but not with Alice. I don't believe a word that stupid witch said to me but that doesn't stop me imagining, through the whole double-PE lesson, that the shuttlecock is Louise's head. Mr Hinch praises my energy and says that I've made real improvement today, and that now he knows what I'm capable of he is going to have higher expectations of me. Fantastic.

During break I go looking for Alice but I can't find her. I'm not too concerned because it's French next, and she's usually forgotten to do her home-work so ends up hiding in a corner of the school somewhere so that she can quickly scribble a few sentences in an attempt to keep Madame Dupont happy. The only thing is, I can't stop thinking about what Louise said.

The minute I walk into the classroom I know that Louise hasn't been lying. Alice is already sitting at our desk but doesn't look at me until I sit down.

'I need to talk to you, Liv,' she says. She looks worried and I start to feel a bit sick and as if maybe I don't want to hear what she's about to say.

'Where were you this morning?' I snap.

'What d'you mean, where was I? You're the one who was late!' she says, looking surprised.

'Whoa, steady on,' I say. 'I only asked! Not my fault my stupid alarm clock broke, is it?'

'Yes, well, don't go blaming me when you're the one who couldn't be bothered to be on time.'

I sit there for a moment, not sure what to say. Why is Alice being so mean to me? She's not even looking at me now, just messing around with the contents of her pencil case.

'Alice?' I say. She ignores me. I have to find out if it's true. 'Hey – you won't believe what totally mental, stupid thing Moronic Louise said to me in PE this morning,' I continue in a pretend-chirpy voice. 'It's the most stupid thing you'll have ever heard. I mean, as if!'

Alice looks at me. 'Everyone's listening – let's talk after class,' she says quietly.

'Is it *true*?' I yell, not caring that the rest of the

class are starting to watch us. 'Has Ben asked *you* out?'

'Please let's not talk about it here, Liv,' whispers Alice, going a funny colour.

'I *knew* it! Well, thanks a lot, Alice – and thanks for letting me hear it from Moronic Louise.' I turn my back on her and try to ignore the attention that we are getting from the people around us.

'Please, Liv,' begs Alice. 'Just listen to me for a minute.'

'Why should I?' I hiss. 'You could at least have told me yourself, not leave me to walk to school on my own. Bet you and *Ben* had a right laugh about that.' I feel a bit ill as I say this, wondering why Alice would do such a thing.

'No!' says Alice, sounding shocked. 'It wasn't like that, I promise. I don't want to have this conversation right now, but meet me after school and we'll sort this out. Please?'

'Whatever,' I say, and busy myself copying the date and the learning objective from the board.

Madame D. walks into the room and everyone reluctantly gets into their seats. I sit in total silence for the rest of the lesson, not moving or saying a word. At one point, it looks like Alice is wiping a tear from her face but I don't care. *What's she got to cry about*, I think. *Nothing, that's what. She obviously doesn't think losing my friendship is very important, so let her cry.*

I get through the rest of the day, sitting alone in maths and science so that I don't have to talk to Alice. Moronic Louise tries to ask me if I'm OK but I snarl at her and even she has the sense to back off. After the longest school day ever, I'm the first to leave the school gates and I run all the way home, desperate not to catch sight of Alice and Ben together.

Mum is lying asleep on the sofa when I slam through the front door.

'Liv?' she calls drowsily. 'Is that you?' I go through to the living room and flop on to the floor next to her. 'What's wrong, sweetheart?' she asks and I tell her everything.

Mum listens and gives me a box of tissues, and hugs me and listens a bit more while I go over and over what went on today. It's a bit hard for her to understand what's actually happened to begin with, cos I'm crying so much that I can't get any words out properly.

'I'll never speak to that disloyal cow again!' I sob when I'm able to make myself understood. 'She doesn't deserve me as her friend.'

'What did Alice actually say happened?' asks Mum, stroking my hair.

'She didn't – I didn't really give her the chance,' I say, taking a deep breath and trying to get a bit of a grip. I actually feel like I might throw up. 'Why would I want to hear a load of lies from her?'

'Has she ever lied to you before?' asks Mum.

'Nooo!' I wail, starting to cry again. 'She's the best friend I've ever had.'

'So, sweetheart, what makes you think she won't tell you the truth if you ask her?'

I haven't really got an answer for that so I think for a bit. 'Well, it wasn't a very honest thing to do, was it? She could have told me herself.'

'But that doesn't mean that she's lied to you, does it?' insists Mum. 'Don't you think that she deserves the chance to talk to you?'

'She *had* her chance, in French.'

'Oh, come on, Liv, you told me yourself that everyone was listening. I bet Alice was really scared about seeing you – people don't always behave their best when they're nervous.'

I think a bit more. 'She's still done a horrible thing, though. She could have told me herself and she must have planned it cos she wasn't waiting for me this morning!'

'You were really late,' Mum reminds me. She sinks back on to the sofa and I can tell she needs to rest. 'You know, one real, true friend is worth more than twenty sort-of friends – and they're worth fighting for. I know what I'm talking about, Liv – I learnt that the hard way when I was your age. Bring me my old diaries and I'll show you.'

I plod upstairs, feeling pretty sure that Mum's diaries are not going to be of any help to me. I don't want to be unkind, but my problem is a little bit more difficult than a dead guinea pig or whether the back door is locked. I get the diaries out from my wardrobe and take them back to Mum. Her eyes are closed when I walk into the room, but she opens them as soon as she hears me and pulls herself up so that she's resting on the cushions.

'Pass them here,' she says, reaching out. I give her the whole lot and then sit down next to her, feeling awful and miserable and completely sorry for myself. Mum skims through the books, muttering stuff like 'No – too young' or 'I can't believe I wrote *that*!' as she reads. The pile of rejected diaries on the floor grows bigger and I zone out for a bit, imagining Alice and Ben laughing about me while heading into town on a date. I don't think it's possible to feel any more terrible than I do right now.

'Here we go,' Mum says suddenly. 'Yes – 1989 started pretty badly for me. I was not a great friend, but I got very, very lucky. Read the entries in January, and remember that you aren't on your own here. I do get it.' She passes me the diary and I put it on top of the others.

Then I snuggle up next to Mum for a while, crying a bit until I don't feel like I want to cry any more. When I can see that she's drifted off to sleep, I stand up and kiss Mum on the head. I pull the blanket that Granny once knitted for her over her legs. Then I go upstairs, carrying the stack of diaries with me. I put them down on my bed and pick up the top book. I might as well read what she has to say after she went to all that trouble to find the right diary. Whatever it is, it obviously stuck in her memory. And actually, I'm a bit curious – I can't imagine Mum being anything other than a great friend.

4 January 1989
Back to school tomorrow - I am NOT looking forward to it at all. I was reading my old diary the other day and saw that a whole year ago I wrote

that if I was going to ever have a boyfriend I'd have one that year. So that's me on the shelf for life then, dying an old spinster with just a few cats to mourn me. So tragic - fourteen years old and no boyfriend. It's embarrassing.

5 January 1989

I don't even know where to start writing this today. I think I might actually be in shock. When I got to school this morning, I couldn't find Beth anywhere. The whole day was rubbish because we usually have a real laugh together and I haven't seen her since the first week of the Christmas holidays. When I came home from school Mum had just got off the phone with Beth's mum. She told me that last week, Beth's mum and dad told Beth that they were splitting up. ANYWAY, the night after they told her, Beth drank loads of stuff from their drinks cabinet - and ended up in hospital. I saw something like this on TV once and they had to pump the girl's stomach. It was totally disgusting.

I wanted to go straight round to Beth's house but Mum said that she wasn't there. She's been sent to stay with her gran and won't be back until the weekend.

I CANNOT believe it. Poor, poor Beth. I wish I could talk to her but I haven't got her gran's number. I hope she rings me soon.

6 January 1989
School was rubbish today. No Beth to hang out with and I didn't really have anyone else to talk to. Hung around with Megan and her crowd for a bit, but they were all talking about a film that they'd watched which was an 18 and I couldn't really join in. There is no way on this earth that I'll ever be allowed to watch an 18 film - even when I'm forty-five, probably.

Beth hasn't phoned me. I'm wondering why she didn't ring me up when her parents told her they were splitting up. We always tell each other everything and she should know that I'm always there for her.

8 January 1989
Wondering where my best friend is? She was meant to be home today but I still haven't heard from her. I cycled past her house but the curtains were all drawn, so I couldn't tell if she was there or not. I know things must be hard for her but she could at least pick up the phone to let me know she's OK.

9 January 1989

Awful, horrible day. I went into school and still no Beth. I was really fed up with being Rachel-no-mates so tried to hang out with Megan's group again. But I wish I hadn't bothered. They started talking about how many boys they've snogged and I could see, if the conversation continued, that I would shortly be called upon to publicly acknowledge my lack of a boyfriend - EVER.

I'm not trying to excuse what I did next but in my defence, it just sort of came out before I knew what I was saying. All I wanted to do was stop them humiliating me in front of the whole school. So I told them about Beth's mum and dad splitting up. And then I told them that she'd been rushed to hospital in an ambulance, after drinking a bottle of sherry.

Everyone was laughing their heads off and I felt bad - but it felt kind of good too, cos I'd made them laugh and they weren't laughing at ME.

And then everyone stopped laughing and went really quiet, and I looked behind me and there was Beth. She looked really pale and wobbly. We stood, looking at each other for a few seconds that felt like a million years, and then she just turned and ran down the corridor. She didn't scream at me or try to pull my hair - I wish she had. She looked so sad and I realized that I'd totally betrayed my best friend in the whole wide world, just so that I could look cool for two minutes to a group of people that I don't even like.

Wow. I cannot imagine Mum behaving like that at all. She never seems to care what other people think. In fact, she's always telling me that the most important thing is to do what *you* want to do, not what other people are doing. And she might be quite embarrassing sometimes but she's never unkind. I'm not sure how I feel about her doing that to Beth – she sounds a bit like one of the mean girls at my school and I bet there's no way that they'll grow up to be as nice and fabulous as my mum.

I'm a bit worried about reading the rest and think that I'll put the diary back in the box. But then I remember that it was Mum who told me to read this bit, so I should probably trust her – and I don't want to disturb her by waking her up right now to check it's OK. I turn the page and continue reading, keeping my fingers crossed that my mum wasn't her school's version of Moronic Louise.

11 January 1989
I have lost my best friend. I don't know what to do.
I tried ringing her up but her mum answered the
phone and said that she was sorry, but Beth didn't
want to speak to me.

Mum came upstairs a while ago and asked me
what was wrong. I've been too ashamed to tell her
what has happened, but it felt good to finally
talk about it. She listened to me and then said
that life isn't about friends who are nice to your
face. It's about friends who are nice behind your
back. I cried quite a lot when she said that, but I
think I know what to do now.

12 January 1989
Went over to Beth's house after school. Nobody
answered the door, but I could see the curtains
move in Beth's room so I kept knocking and yelling
up at her window. I said that I wasn't going to
leave until she talked to me.

I sat on her front step for what felt like
hours, but was probably about ten minutes, and
then her mum walked up the drive. She asked why I
was sitting on her step. I told her that I was really
sorry and that I needed to tell Beth properly. She
said she'd see what she could do and went inside.

I sat there for another ten minutes, and then the front door opened and Beth came out with two mugs of hot chocolate.

We sat next to each other for a bit and then I told her how sorry I was and what a terrible friend I'd been and how, if she forgave me, I'd never, ever behave like that again. She told me to shut up and drink my hot chocolate. We gave each other a hug and I told her what my mum had said and promised that from now on, I would be the sort of friend who was always nice behind her back and that I'd always defend her and be here for her.

We both cried a bit and laughed a bit, and then Beth said that HER mum always quotes some Sicilian proverb about how only your real friends will tell you when your face is dirty. And that I had hot chocolate smeared all around my mouth.

I close Mum's diary with a sigh of relief – my mum was nothing like Louise. She's never told me all that about Beth before, though, and she and Beth are still good friends to this day, so she must have done something right. I think over what *their* mums told them about friendship, and why Mum told me to read this today, and I know that

I have not been a true friend to Alice. Sure, I'm mad at her, but I didn't actually give her the chance to tell me what had happened and that isn't very fair.

The phone starts ringing and straight away I know it's her. She's about the only person that rings our house – Isaac hasn't got any friends and Mum and Dad get most of their phone calls on their mobiles. I've been on at them for ages to let me have a mobile but they've always got an excuse. First I was too young, then they said it'd cost too much – Mum even tried telling me that it could give me brain damage. I tried to tell her that being the only person in my whole, entire school without a mobile phone was definitely damaging my health, but she wasn't convinced. Anyway, Alice and I have never let an argument carry on to the next day and I know that Alice won't be able to relax until she's spoken to me. I want to talk with her too – but I still feel like making her wait a bit longer. After all, she knows how I feel about Ben.

'Liv!' Isaac shouts up the stairs. He's just started answering the phone and takes the whole procedure extremely seriously. 'Alice is on the phone. She wants to talk to you.'

'Tell her I'm out!' I yell back.

'But you're not out. You're in. I can hear you,' calls Isaac. I sigh deeply. Not only do I now have to talk to Alice; she'll have heard all of that little exchange cos there is no way that Isaac will have used the mute button.

I stomp down the stairs and Isaac hands me the phone, but not before saying, 'I *knew* you were in!' in a triumphant manner. I take a deep breath.

'Hi,' I say, as frostily as I can.

'Liv, please just listen to me and don't hang up!' Alice jabbers in a garbled rush. Hang up on her? When have I ever hung up on her? The girl's been watching way too much television. 'I'm really sorry, Liv. I really don't want to lose you as my best friend.'

'So – *are* you going out with Ben?' I ask her.

'No!' Alice sounds shocked.

'But you didn't wait for me this morning and you walked into school with him?'

'Well, yes – but it wasn't like that, Liv.'

'What was it like then?' I say, still feeling hurt. I know I was horrible to Alice in class but she hasn't exactly acted like my best friend. 'Did you just end up ditching me for him by mistake?'

'Liv – that's what I wanted to talk to you about! I was waiting and waiting for you this morning and you didn't turn up. Ben was just walking past on the way to school, so we ended up walking in together cos I thought you must be off, ill. Then just as we got into school Louise and her cronies saw us and started saying "Ooh, new boyfriend, Alice?", and I was really embarrassed and Ben looked utterly horrified and ran off and – well, you know the rest!'

'So you weren't going out with him yesterday?'

'No!'

'And you didn't plan to leave me to walk to school on my own this morning?'

'Definitely not!'

'And you're not actually going out with him now?'

'No,' says Alice in a bored voice.

'And you didn't tell Moronic Louise something before you told me?'

'Liv!' Alice actually sounds quite fed up now. 'What do you take me for? I would never tell her anything. I wouldn't tell her the time – so how on earth could you think that I would tell her any-thing of actual importance?'

'Sorry,' I mutter.

'Not that there was anything to tell, you do understand,' demands Alice.

'Yeah – I get that now,' I say, trying to sound as apologetic as possible.

'But when, or if, I ever have any important information of any kind, I can promise you that you'll be the first to find out. OK?'

'OK,' I say.

'And I would never, ever, *ever* go out with a boy that you like cos that would be all kinds of wrong.'

'I know. Me neither,' I whisper, feeling a bit ashamed.

There's a pause and then Alice starts laughing. 'What a rubbish day! Can it be over now?'

'It really can,' I tell her. 'In fact – that's it. All done. I'm going straight upstairs to put my pyjamas on.'

'Me too!' she says. 'Then I'm going to curl up on the sofa and watch –'

'*The Simpsons!*' I interrupt.

'Of course!' Alice says.

'See you tomorrow then,' I say, smiling down the phone.

'Usual place?'

'Usual place,' I agree.

'Bye then – and Liv?'

'Yeah?'

'Put a new battery in your alarm clock, OK?'

'Deal,' I say. 'Bye, Alice!'

When I put the phone down and turn round, I see that Mum is standing in the kitchen doorway. I grin at her.

'All sorted?' she asks me.

'Yes,' I tell her. 'I shouldn't have been so quick to get mad with Alice. I kind of leapt to the wrong conclusion, but we're OK now.'

'She's a good friend,' says Mum.

'The best,' I agree, taking her arm and leading her back to the sofa. 'She'd definitely tell me if my face was dirty!'

Mum smiles at me. 'Ahh – so the diaries *have* been a bit useful!'

'I'm never going to be mean to Alice ever again. It just made me feel horrible and look stupid,' I say. 'I want me and Alice to be friends for as long as you and Beth have been friends.'

I tuck Mum back in and try to make her cosy. She's been getting really cold the last few days, and no matter how many blankets we pile on her, she still shivers and shakes. I can feel that her hot water bottle has cooled down so I pick it up and go into the kitchen.

'I hope you'll get to have a longer friendship with Alice than I have with Beth,' I hear her say quietly. 'A friendship that lasts a proper lifetime, not just half of one.'

I don't think I'm supposed to have heard that so I don't reply, but I realize that today, I've almost enjoyed having something else to think about. I wonder if I'd have got so mad at Alice if Mum wasn't – well, doing what she's doing. I think that I wouldn't have been so upset, that's for sure.

And I realize that I am going to need Alice more than I've ever needed her before and that maybe it's time to tell her what's happening in my house.

Two Weeks Before

I walk into the kitchen to see Dad and Isaac updating the wall planner on the wall. Like the one in his bedroom, it shows Isaac all the things that will be happening this week so that he can be prepared. Unlike the one in his bedroom, this wall planner charts all of Mum's hospital appointments so that Isaac knows when she won't be at home. And so that he can start to understand that she's really, truly ill.

Ever since that horrible evening when Mum and Dad told us that Mum was properly ill I've been waiting for Isaac to have a total meltdown, but it hasn't happened. I asked Dad about it the other day and he said that he doesn't think Isaac is letting the information through – that it's a bit like him closing a gate in his mind to stop him from thinking about things that will upset him.

Lucky Isaac, I said. I wish I didn't have to think about it either.

Since I said this, Dad has been working really hard to keep telling Isaac about how Mum is doing and what each appointment is for. I think he's worried that Isaac will lose it for good if he doesn't start talking about it with us soon.

I grab some cornflakes and take a look at the new schedule. Mum is going to be pretty busy this week – she has hospital appointments almost every day.

'Can you make sure that you're home on time after school today?' Dad asks me, washing a couple of apples and putting them in our lunchboxes. 'I need to drive Mum back from seeing the doctor and we'll be a bit late.'

'Sure,' I say. Isaac's special school is quite a few miles away so he has to have a taxi there and back – which is a good thing because it means that he's never the first person home at the end of the day. 'How's Mum feeling today?'

'Not so good,' says Dad. 'She didn't really get any sleep again last night.'

I look over at him, worried. He doesn't sound his normal, cheery self this morning.

'But the doctors will be able to help her, won't

they?' I ask. 'Just tell them to give her something that'll help her sleep. Alice said her mum has pills to help her go to sleep all the time.'

'Yes, well – it's not quite the same thing, I'm afraid,' says Dad, handing me my lunch.

'But there's still hope, isn't there?' I say. 'You said that technology is improving constantly and that it's simply a question of trying everything until something works.'

Dad doesn't say anything, just looks at me and runs his fingers through his hair. 'Dad? You *said* that, remember?'

'I remember, Liv. The thing is – your mum's tried nearly everything now.'

I take a huge breath of relief. 'Well, there you go then! *Nearly* everything isn't everything, is it? Make sure they do *everything* they can, Dad – you have to!'

'I will, Liv. And your mum's determined to fight this thing – and you know what she's like when she sets her mind to something.'

I love Dad for trying to lighten the mood, but I can feel that something has changed. My heart starts to race and my armpits feel prickly with sweat.

'Dad?' I ask him, but I can't finish my sentence.

I don't even know what the rest of the sentence might be, just that it's so bad I can't find the words to say it or even think it.

Dad moves round the kitchen table and squeezes my shoulder. 'We need to sit down, Liv – have a chat.'

'No!' I say, the word coming out louder than I expected. 'It's fine, Dad – really. You don't need to worry – I'll be here for Isaac after school.'

My gaze falls again on the wall planner with Mum's hospital appointments crowding out the rest of the month. Dad follows my eyes to see where I'm looking and squeezes my shoulder again.

'We'll talk when I get back later,' he tells me. He tries to smile at me but while his mouth turns up at each corner, his eyes don't seem to get the message, and when I leave the kitchen he is still standing there, looking at the wall planner with his pretend, everything's-going-to-be-OK Dad smile on his face. I can feel that I need to make doubly certain that I am here when Isaac gets home from school. And I can feel that it is time to stop acting like a little girl and take some responsibility.

The first thing that I do with my newfound mature and responsible self is to bunk off school. It is so

ludicrously easy to do that I can't believe I haven't
ever done it before. I say goodbye to Mum and
Dad and walk down to our corner where Alice is
waiting for me. I'm going to tell her my plan and
ask her to cover for me at school. To be honest, I
think she'll agree to just about anything I ask her
right now. I told her about Mum the other day –
she cried for ages. All this week she's made sure
that Moronic Louise doesn't get anywhere near
me – and school's been a little bit easier now that
she knows. We haven't actually talked about it
since, but it feels a bit like I've got some back-up
now.

'Hey, Liv.' Alice is already waiting at the corner,
waving at me. I walk towards her and when I
reach her I drop my bag on the pavement and
lean back against the wall. Alice looks at me in
surprise but doesn't say a word, just drops her
own bag and leans back next to me, one foot
resting on the wall behind us.

'I can't go to school,' I tell her.

'Why? What's happened?' Alice is panicking
and her voice comes out all high and breathless.
'Liv? Has your mum –'

'No!' I say, wrapping my arms across my body
and shivering a little. 'Nothing's changed.'

'Thank God for that.' Alice slumps a little and I can tell how scared she is. 'I thought –'

'I know,' I tell her and we stand in silence for a minute, watching the cars go past.

'Life is so totally rubbish,' Alice says eventually. 'I never knew it could be this unfair. I just can't stop thinking about your mum. Why can't you go to school?'

'It's wasting time,' I say. I'm not sure how else to tell her what I'm feeling, but I just know there are far more important things to do today than go to school.

'Are you going to stay at home with your mum?' asks Alice, and I know that she wants to understand; that she's trying to make sense of what is happening. I don't have the energy to explain that Mum will be at the hospital most of today and that I feel like I'm missing something. I can't put into words how it felt when Dad said we needed to 'have a talk'.

'Yes,' I tell her. It seems easier somehow, and I'm not completely sure myself why I know that I have to stay at home today.

'OK,' says Alice. 'Give your mum a big hug from me. Tell her my mum said to just ask if she needs anything. Tell her –' But her voice chokes up and she stops talking, rubbing at her eyes and trying to hide the tears that are welling up inside them.

'I'll tell her. Cover for me at school?'

Alice nods and gives me a hug, and then runs down the road while I go the other way and nip down the alleyway that is at the back of our garden. Normally I'll do anything to avoid this alley. Nothing bad has ever happened there as far as I know, but it makes me think about death and dog poo – not my favourite subjects. I know that Mum and Dad are meant to be leaving quite early so I hang around at the end of the alley for a bit, enjoying the early morning sun, until I reckon they'll have gone and then I leave the sunshine and head down the shadowy pathway.

The wall is quite high, so I have a bit of trouble judging which bit of the alley is next to our garden. When I think I'm close I drag a dustbin up to the wall – good job that (a) it's bin day, and (b) the bin men have already emptied the dustbins – and stand on it. Well, I say that like it's easy. Actually, it's quite difficult to stand up on a bin. They're always doing it on telly but on reflection, I think they must film that bit with stunt doubles because it takes me *ages* to balance myself on top. And then, when I can finally see over the wall, I see that it's not even *our* garden – I'm still three doors down, about to jump into Mrs Green's immaculate flower bed. She's always been really lovely to me but even so, I don't think she'd be very happy if she spotted me trampling all over her plants.

I get down (about as easy as getting up there) and repeat the whole charade – this time in the right place. Bizarrely, clambering over the garden wall is the easy bit. I just sort of pull myself up on to my tummy and then slowly tip my whole body over. Not very elegant – no points for my dismount, but effective all the same.

I pick myself up and brush myself down, and then creep round the back of Dad's studio and let myself in with the key that he imaginatively hides under a flowerpot.

There, on my bench, are the rubbish photographs that I took on my birthday. I've gathered up photos that I took months ago with my old camera too – they're all here. I look at them now, choosing quickly and putting them into two piles. When I'm done, I sweep the second pile into a drawer and then, taking the rest, I spread them out all over Dad's huge table.

Now I can take my time, picking up each image and looking at it properly, holding it to the light and turning it this way and that. I discard a few more pictures and I sort the rest into another two groups. When I'm done, I stand back and look.

Staring up at me from the table is Mum. Lots and lots of photographs of my mum. I gather up the first collection and flick through. In one frame she's got her arm round Dad and is laughing at something he's said. In another, Isaac is pushing her on a swing in the park and her hair is fanning out behind her and her legs are straight out in front of her, and she's smiling and smiling. A third shows her sitting at the kitchen table, glasses pushed up on her head and a frown of concentration on her face, as she writes an article that is probably due in the next day. What all of these pictures have in common is they show how Mum lives every day – like it really, really matters.

The next lot of photos are more recent. They're the photos that I took of my birthday tea and in the few weeks before my birthday, and they still show my mum – but she's not the same. She's still laughing and hugging in these pictures but she looks *so* different. I can't believe I haven't noticed before. How come I can see it on a photo but not in real life?

I put all the pictures back on the table and spread them out again. Frantically, I start to order them chronologically, trying to remember when I took each one. When they're all lined up in order, I step back and look at the timeline I've created. I look from left to right, as my mum seems to shrink in size. The photos on the left show a mum who was easy to hug, who was never overweight but was definitely cuddly. They show a mum who was quick to get mad and quick to forgive and quick to laugh at everything life threw at her.

The photos on the right side of my timeline show a new mum. This one is thin and could do with eating some chocolate; this one wants to hug you but you worry that you might break her, she feels so brittle. This mum seems to be watching everything that goes on around her instead of joining in, and she looks like that is killing her.

I turn away from the table and stifle a sob. I do not want to cry right now. Tears would be totally pointless. How did I not notice, I rage inside my head. I thought she was getting better. I thought this would all be over – I knew it might take a bit of time, but I thought we'd get there in the end. I've even found myself getting cross with her, wishing that she wasn't spoiling everything by being unwell.

I picture our wall planner in the kitchen and see how Mum has been visiting the hospital more and more frequently. The evidence was there, right in front of me all the time. All I had to do was look but I chose not to. Maybe I'm more like Isaac than I realized. I wonder if one day, these photographs will be the only evidence that she was ever here, that she ever actually existed.

I'm not sure how long I've been in the studio but I'm suddenly really freezing. It's weird cos it looks like it's turning into quite a nice day outside, but I'm actually shaking, I'm so cold. I think about what I should do now. I leave the studio, walk down the garden path to the back door and find the key (yet again, imaginatively placed under a flowerpot). I go inside and put the kettle on, amazed at how calm I am. I feel nothing inside, just a big, empty hole – and I hope it stays like that because the idea of feeling anything is unbearable.

Just as the kettle boils I hear the click of the front door opening and a second later, the sound of it closing. I turn my head slowly towards the kitchen doorway. Presumably I'm going to have to explain to Dad why I'm not at school and my brain seems to have stopped working, which is a problem because I will need a good excuse in approximately two seconds.

I hear footsteps coming down the hallway and pause. I can't actually see anything because there's suddenly something wrong with my eyes – water is flowing out of them and I can't make it stop. I blink hard and rub them and when I look up, it isn't Dad standing there at all.

I run across the room and she meets me halfway, scooping me up in a big hug that I never want to end.

'It's OK, Livvy, it's OK,' she whispers. 'I'm here now, you can let it all go.'

I realize that I'm crying and that now I've started I might actually not ever stop. But I have to stop because I have to say the words – even though I know that once I've said them they can never be unsaid. I pull back from her and look her squarely in the eye.

'It's not OK, Aunt Leah. It's never going to be OK again. Don't you understand?'

She doesn't break my eye contact but reaches out her hand and holds on to my arm, as if she understands that all of a sudden, I feel like I'm a kite that might just disappear on a strong gust of air if somebody doesn't tether me to them.

'Do you know?' I ask her, suddenly scared that she might not and that I might be called upon to be brave for her. She nods slightly but stays quiet, and I know she realizes that I need to speak the words myself.

'I only knew for sure just now,' I tell her. 'How did I not know before?'

'Maybe you weren't ready to know before,' she says, still looking at me.

'I'm not ready to know *now*,' I wail. 'I don't want to know. I shouldn't have to know something like this.'

I can't look at her any more and she pulls me back into her arms, holding me tightly against her.

'Make it go away – make it be all right.' I'm hoping that maybe Leah can think of the answer – something that'll fix this.

'I can't, Livvy,' Leah says.

'So it's really going to happen then?' I ask, feeling the last, tiny burst of hope explode in my stomach.

'Yes,' she says, and the hope is extinguished, leaving only the empty hole.

'My mum is really going to die,' I whisper.

'Yes, my darling girl, she is,' Leah whispers back.

I stand in our kitchen for a long time and it gets so I'm not sure whether I'm holding on to Leah or she's holding on to me. My legs start to hurt and my eyes are sore, and I know that I need to move but I'm scared to let go in case the whole world has shattered into tiny pieces while I was crying. Leah makes the decision for me, moving me towards the table and guiding me into a chair.

'What your mum always recommends in times of need is a big slab of chocolate,' she says, and heads towards the kitchen cupboards. 'I've lost count of the number of times she's listened to me and sorted me out and put the world to rights over a decent chunk of rich, dark chocolate.' I can hear a catch in her voice and I look up anxiously to see if she's crying, but she looks across at me and gives a reassuring smile.

'Why aren't you crying?' I ask her, sniffing loudly. I know that, despite Mum's accounts in her diaries of Leah when they were children, they're really close now, always nattering on the phone to each other and arranging weekends away.

'I've done a whole heap of crying – and I'll do a whole heap more, I know, but right now, I'm all cried out,' she says, handing me a box of tissues. 'Besides, I haven't come here to cry, have I? I've come to look after my naughty, skiving niece!'

That gets me thinking, which seems to help stem the tears a little. This is a good thing because my crying seems to have taken on a life of its own and I really wouldn't mind a few minutes off, just to think about something else. My head is throbbing and my eyes are stinging – even my nose feels sore and I'm not sure why that is.

'Why *are* you here? I thought you were meant to be coming at the weekend? It's only Monday.'

'I'm quite aware of what day it is, young lady. As my boss will be when I phone him up later. And as for *why* I'm here – I told you, to make sure you're OK.' She passes me a cup of tea and sits down opposite.

'But I'm supposed to be in school,' I say, confused now.

'Exactly! Fancy bunking off on a Monday – even I used to wait until Friday afternoon. And your mum never skived a single day. You'll be in so much trouble when she walks through that door, I can tell you *that* for nothing!' Leah actually looks like she's enjoying herself for a minute, and despite everything, I can't help grinning.

'But how did you know I wasn't in school?' I ask her. 'I thought you had a proper job – or are my parents employing you to spy on me?'

'Hahaha – or should that be LOL? I had no idea that you weren't where you were supposed to be – until I had a phone call from your father at ten past nine this morning, asking me to hotfoot it over here and keep an eye on you.'

'Dad?'

'Yes.'

'Dad rang you?'

'Yes, Liv.'

'To say I was skiving?'

'Crikey – you catch on quick, don't you?'

'He *knew* I was here? How?'

She smiles at me. 'He saw you throwing yourself over the garden wall. Actually, he heard what he described as "a terrible racket" in the alley and went upstairs to see if he could catch sight of whoever was dragging his bin down the path. Imagine his surprise when your sweet little head popped up over the wall!'

I gawp at her, speechless.

'He kept watching to make sure you survived the landing and saw you go into the studio. He said you'd had a difficult start to the day and figured that you could do with a day off.'

I still can't say anything. I am silenced by the knowledge that my dad knew where I was the whole time – and left me alone to sort stuff out without telling me off for skiving.

'One last thing, Liv?' says Leah.

'Yes?' I mumble.

'He asked me to tell you not to bother applying for any jobs at MI5 – he says stealth-like actions are not your forte!' Leah tries to keep a straight face but fails. She starts laughing and I join in. The weird thing about laughing, though, is that it uses exactly the same parts of your body that you use when you cry, so we both stop quite quickly in case the crying takes over again.

'I was coming over tonight or tomorrow anyway,' she says, serious again now. 'Your dad could do with the help and I need to get to grips with how you guys do things around here. Don't want to go upsetting Isaac by giving him the wrong spoon!'

We smile at each other, but are back in the real

world again now. The real world, where Leah coming to stay at the weekend could be too late. Where tomorrow might belong to a different life – a life that I wish, with every bit of me, was not going to be mine.

One Week Before

Mum has gone.

The house feels totally different and not really like our house at all. Dad keeps saying that she's only on the other side of town and we can visit her every day after school if we want to – but even he can't pretend that it's the same.

We've come to see her today. Dad has been before but it's the first time Isaac and I have been here, and as soon as Dad stops the car I know that it's going to be awful. I hang back, pretending I've lost something down the back of the car seat and hoping that Dad will just take Isaac in without me.

No such luck.

'Come on, Liv,' he says, a bit impatiently.

I am totally not in the mood for him to have a go at me right now so I stay where I am.

'Liv,' he says again, with a warning in his voice.

He's been a total grouch the last few days and majorly bossy. I can tell he's not going to let me stay behind so I drag myself out of the car, as slowly as I dare – I want him to know that this is not OK with me but I don't really want to start an argument.

'What's the big rush anyway?' I grumble. 'It's not like she's going anywhere.' I can hear my voice sounding even grumpier than Dad's. I'm actually not in a bad mood but I am feeling a bit scared.

'Mum's been waiting for us, Liv – she wants to hear all about your day,' says Dad as he locks the door and puts a hand on my shoulder, propelling me along the path after Isaac.

And straight away I feel horrid and guilty. I raise my eyes and take a proper look at the building in front of us. It looks like the sort of house that a really posh family would live in – I can imagine it at Christmas, all lit up with lamps in every window and a couple of expensive cars on the driveway. I bet there's a massive hallway where they'd put a gigantic Christmas tree, covered in candles and silver tinsel – totally the opposite of our Christmas tree that is usually leaning over to one side and dripping with multicoloured fairy lights and about a million tacky decorations, made by me and Isaac when we were little. Mum is utterly incapable of throwing anything like that away, so every year our poor tree spends the Christmas holidays smothered with cardboard angels and sheep made out of empty loo-roll tubes. Dad always says it looks like a car crash of a Christmas tree, but Mum just laughs and tells him not to be such a Scrooge.

I look around as we walk up the path. Everything is very neat and tidy. It doesn't look like any children ever play in this garden, which is a shame, cos I can see an excellent tree for climbing and a little stream and a huge weeping willow with branches that reach right down to the ground – I bet there's room for a little secret den inside there. It's the sort of place where I could take hundreds of photographs, but I haven't felt like using my camera since my birthday. Nothing seems important enough any more for me to record it. I used to think that the whole world was full of amazing things that could leap out at me and take me by surprise – wonderful moments that I'd want to remember forever. Now I hate surprises and instead of wondering 'why' when I stop to take a photo, I just wonder 'why bother?' It's not as if you can take a photograph with you when you go.

'Liv?' says Dad, and I realize that he's been talking to me. 'Come on, let's go and find Mum's room. I know she's desperate to see you.'

We walk up the steps and in through the open front door. The massive hall is just as I imagined it. But there's no Christmas tree, and even though I knew that there wouldn't be – it's only April, for goodness' sake – I can't help feeling a little disappointed.

Dad leads us up the stairs. He's been to visit Mum every day so he knows where we need to go, and I'm glad that he seems confident because I'm feeling really nervous.

I've missed Mum so much since we found out that she was ill. It's weird, but I started missing her when she was still in the house – it felt like she wasn't really there the way that she used to be. And then, last week, everything went downhill. Mum couldn't really get out of bed, and when I went in to say 'hello' to her after school each afternoon she was either asleep or lying very still, and wouldn't say very much. She didn't smell right either – not like Mum. I was too scared to ask her why. I thought she might not have noticed and I didn't want to hurt her feelings. Sometimes she wanted me to lie down next to her and have a hug, but I didn't really want to cos she didn't feel like Mum and the odd smell thing totally bothered me – I don't know why. It just felt like cuddling a stranger.

Dad took the week off work and spent the whole time racing around – trying to get Mum to eat, carrying her to the bathroom or talking on the phone to the doctors at the hospital. Leah was in charge of looking after me and Isaac, which meant that I spent the whole week trying to avoid Isaac meltdowns. It was hard work cos even though he loves Leah, he didn't like the fact that everything was different, and Dad was too busy with Mum to help Isaac understand what was going on. I did my best but I didn't really know what to tell him either, so we just kind of muddled through.

Last Thursday I woke up in the middle of the night and thought I'd check on Mum after I'd been to the loo. But before I could open her bedroom door I heard the sound of crying. And it wasn't Mum doing the crying. I don't think I've ever heard my dad cry before and I hope I never, ever hear that again. I wanted to run back to bed and pretend that I hadn't heard, but for some reason my feet wouldn't move so I had to stay, with my head resting on the door, listening. I think

I cried a bit too, but I'm not sure if I was crying for me, Mum or Dad.

On Friday morning Dad told us that he was taking Mum to stay here, in St Mary's Hospice. He said they could make her more comfortable than he could at home. I've heard that word a lot this week and it always makes me want to laugh. Slippers are comfortable; our old sofa is comfortable, but I could never describe my mum as 'comfortable'. She's always too busy and energetic and exciting to be a word like that. She'd be pretty narked off if she thought someone was calling her 'comfortable' – she hates lame words like 'nice' and 'lovely' and 'pretty', and I know for a fact that she'd say 'comfortable' is definitely a lame word.

We're standing outside a closed door now and I know that this must be Mum's room. My heart starts beating faster and I can feel my armpits starting to prickle with sweat. What if she doesn't look like Mum any more? Just how ill is she right now? Or even worse, is she going to be in pain? The idea of my mum hurting is more than I can begin to deal with and I take a step backwards – they can't actually *make* me go in, can they? I'm thinking that the little secret den under the weeping willow tree would be a pretty good place to hide, and I picture myself curled up on the ground watching the sunlight coming through gaps in the leaves, and the damp, fresh smell of the earth, and nobody in the world knowing where I am or asking me to do something that I cannot possibly do.

But then Dad is opening the door.

'Just act normally, Liv,' he says, then disappears inside, and I have no choice but to dumbly follow him and Isaac – all the time wishing that I was a stronger person, with enough strength to turn round and run away.

I'm surprised when I step inside the room. It's bigger than I expected and the late afternoon sun is streaming through a huge window that over-looks the front drive and the car park. There are two beds and there, sitting in front of the window on a chair, is Mum. I realize she must have been watching out for us and I hope she couldn't tell that I didn't want to get out of the car.

Dad has rushed over to Mum and is hugging her and whispering in her ear. I can't hear what he says but a big smile spreads across her face. Isaac has been hanging back, looking worried, but when Dad pulls away, Isaac walks carefully across the room and gives Mum a gentle pat on the arm. She stretches her arm round him and rubs the small of his back and Isaac relaxes a bit, sitting down on the edge of Mum's bed and turning his iPod on. He's in his own world now, where he doesn't have to think about what we're doing here.

Mum looks across at me. I can't take my eyes off her. She looks like Mum but I'm still not sure whether it's really OK to act as if everything's normal. I mean, this is totally *not* normal. It's nothing like normal. I really want her to cuddle me – in fact, I want it more than anything else in the world right now, but I'm so scared of getting it wrong and I just don't know what to do.

I stand there, by the door, for a few seconds that feel like a few hours, and then Mum opens her arms and nods her head at me, smiling. And just like that, I know it's OK because she's told me that it is. I run across the room and throw myself on to her lap. I haven't sat on her knee for years now and I don't want to hurt her, but I really need this; I want to feel like I used to when I was a little girl – when I thought my mum would always be there for me and would always protect me and never leave me, no matter what. Her arms tighten round me, and I rest my head on her shoulder and breathe in deeply – and even if she doesn't smell the way she always has, she smells like my mum smells now and that's fine with me.

We sit like this for a while and I'm not sure if I'm holding on to Mum or she's holding on to me, and it doesn't really matter because while we're cuddled up together I can remember all the really good stuff.

I think of the way she tucks me into bed at night, even though I'm probably a bit old for that now. I think about how she taught me to swim, standing for hours in the freezing-cold kids' pool and not complaining every time I kicked water in her face. I remember the times we've sat round our kitchen table playing card games, she and Dad getting really competitive and laughing like crazy, and me and Isaac knowing that if we kept quiet then they'd forget it was supposed to be bedtime half an hour ago. I think how she always tells me the truth, even if it's really hard to hear. I think about how she always loves me, even when I'm in a grotty, horrible mood. She knows everything about me – all the good stuff and all the bad stuff – and she never, ever stops loving me, and I know this is what I am most scared of losing. I wonder if anyone will ever love me again the way that my mum loves me, and I know that nobody ever can – it would be impossible. And that is so awful a thought that I have to stop thinking before I get sucked down into a place that I can't come back from.

After a while, I feel Mum shifting beneath me and I realize I'm too heavy for her. I get up and sit next to Isaac on her bed.

'So how was school today?' asks Mum.

'Fine,' I say. I look over at Dad in amazement – are we really going to talk about boring stuff like school, as if nothing big is happening here? Dad smiles encouragingly at me and I remember that Mum has been sitting in this room waiting for us all day. I try to make a bit more of an effort.

'I got a detention for not doing my history homework and I came last in the cross-country run in PE.'

Dad frowns at me but Mum laughs. 'Oh well, you can't be brilliant at everything! Get Dad to help you with your history – he's quite a mine of information when you get him started.'

'How was your day, Rachel?' asks Dad, reaching out to take hold of one of Mum's hands.

'Oh – you know, same old, same old!' jokes Mum, smiling a big smile that doesn't look quite real. I feel I should be doing better at this and cast my eyes around the room, looking for something to start a conversation about.

'Your room's nice?' I offer, hoping it's OK to talk about where we are.

'Yes, I'm really lucky, aren't I?' says Mum, looking pleased. 'The nurses tell me it's one of the sunnier rooms.'

'You've got loads of space. It's much bigger than your room at home,' I tell her, feeling a bit braver. I can do this – I can sit here and just chat about nothing.

Mum smiles. 'I've put the photo that you sent me on the noticeboard over there – can you see it?'

'Oh!' I go a bit red. 'It's rubbish! I'll find a better one when I get home, I promise.' I'm feeling really embarrassed and mean. Dad wanted me to choose a photograph of us all for him to bring in for Mum the other day, but I spent ages talking on the phone to Alice and then I wanted to watch TV, so I just grabbed the first one I could find and it wasn't a good choice. It was taken at some wildlife park – Isaac isn't looking at the camera, Mum looks seriously fed up and half of Dad is obscured by someone who was walking past. I look pretty good – but that's only because I quite liked the boy that Dad asked to take our photo and I was doing my best smile. It wasn't even a particularly good day out. It poured with rain and we got lost on the way there, which meant Mum and Dad moaned at each other for about an hour and then promised (yet again) to buy each other a satnav for their next wedding anniversary. Dad didn't say a word when I gave that photo to him, though, so I thought I'd got away with it – and to be honest, I couldn't really be bothered. Now I'm wishing I'd tried harder and found Mum a photo that reminds her how happy we used to be.

'That picture's fine, Liv – I love it,' says Mum.

Isaac is still listening to his music and Dad is skimming through a leaflet on counselling services. I'm keen to get off this conversation and on to a subject that's easier to talk about – something that doesn't make me feel bad.

'It's good that you've got a room all to yourself,' I say, 'although I suppose it might be quite nice to share too. You could have midnight feasts – like a sleepover for adults!'

'I suppose you could,' Mum says.

'So how come there's nobody in that other bed?' I say, pointing to the spare bed opposite. 'I thought Dad said there was another lady in your room?'

This is something I'd been really worried about before we came to visit Mum. Dad had said she'd made friends with a lady who was already in the room that Mum was put in – and that she was being kind to Mum and telling her all about St Mary's, showing her photos of her kids and asking Mum all about us. Dad said that it was good for Mum to have someone else to talk to. I didn't want to see someone else who was ill, though – ill people always make me feel a bit funny (not funny ha-ha but funny weird), and I was scared that Mum would make me talk to her new friend and I might say the wrong thing or do something stupid. So I'm really glad that the other bed in Mum's room is stripped bare with just a plain pillow at the top and a stack of sheets and blankets folded neatly at the bottom.

I look at Mum. 'Has she gone somewhere else?' I ask.

Mum opens her mouth to speak but doesn't actually say anything. She looks at Dad and I can see she's worried. She's not smiling any more and the room suddenly feels different. I can tell that something isn't right and I'm desperate to keep Mum talking – last week at home she barely said a word. I want her to smile again so I try to make her laugh.

'Did she get fed up with you snoring in your sleep and ask to be moved?' I say, grinning and waiting for Mum to tell me not to be so cheeky, but she still doesn't say a word.

'Mum?' I ask.

'Liv,' starts Dad, but I interrupt him. I don't like the way it feels as if things are going a bit weird.

'Where's the lady that Dad says is your friend? Did you fall out with her?' I can hear myself asking stupid questions and feel panic rising in my chest. I want to stop talking but I can't. I don't want to give Dad a chance to say something that I really, really do not want to hear. 'Was she not very nice after all? She wasn't mean to you, was she?'

'It's nothing like that, Liv,' says Mum very quietly. 'Her name was Joanna and she was an amazing lady. We had lots of great chats about our children and she said some things that have helped me very much.'

'So where is she now?' I ask, then instantly regret asking such a terrible question. Now I can't stop them telling me. I'm so stupid. I'm wishing I'd never started this conversation – it's all gone wrong.

'Liv,' says Dad again. I look at him and he is

sitting really stiffly in his chair, looking uneasy, which seems funny in a place that goes on and on about making people comfortable. Looking at him makes me want to laugh even though I've never felt less amused in my whole life, and there are giggles building up in my throat. But it doesn't feel very nice and I swallow hard, thinking I'd better not start laughing cos it seems like I might not be able to stop. It feels as if I could actually laugh myself to death right now.

'Joanna has moved on,' he says.

'Yes, that's what I'm asking. Where has she moved on to?' I say, hoping that he'll shut up if I'm deliberately difficult.

There is a long pause. I look again at the empty bed – Joanna's bed – and I can't keep pretending. I can feel my tummy start to shrivel and shrink as all my muscles knot up tightly. I suddenly don't feel like laughing any more.

No. No, no, no. I look at Mum, hoping that I've put two and two together and made eighteen. Hoping that I'm actually completely wrong. 'What – she's actually –' I can't say the word. I am so thick and this conversation is *not* happening. In my mind I am under the weeping willow tree, with my fingers rammed firmly in my ears and humming loudly to drown out all the terrible thoughts that are flying round my head right now.

Mum takes a deep breath and sits up a bit straighter. 'Yes, love. It's very sad but Joanna –'

'Stop!' I shout. I can't say that word and I don't want to hear anyone else say it either.

'Liv – I know it's hard but she was incredibly brave. I really admired her.'

'But she had kids,' I whisper, feeling utterly horrified.

'Yes, three children. The older two are around your age and the youngest is eight.'

'That's horrible,' I mutter, unable to look at Mum or Dad.

I feel stupid and angry with myself. How could I be so dense? How could I let this conversation happen? Let's be honest – I know exactly what this place is. It's not about head massages or three different choices of breakfast. It's not about sunny rooms or large gardens or chatting to new friends. It's the place where people go to die. My mum is here, waiting in line for her turn – and some time soon her bed will be empty, the book she's reading and her hairbrush will have gone from the bedside table and my rubbish photo will have been taken down from the noticeboard, as if it was never there. There might even be another person in her bed – maybe another mum who will tell her family all about this wonderful woman that she had the privilege of meeting.

'Rachel Ellis,' she'll say. 'That was her name. So young but so courageous.' And her kids will silently be willing her to keep quiet, not wanting to be part of a world where someone's mum can be taken away from her children when they need her.

And I realize that I don't want Mum to be brave. I want her to rant and shout. I want her to scream about the unfairness of it all and jump up and down and yell at doctors and *fight*. Most of all I want her to fight. Because deep down I'm sure that my powerful, bossy, controlling mum could beat this if only she would try a little bit harder. Being here feels like she's given up – that she's quietly shuffling forward in a pair of comfortable slippers to a place where we can't go.

I stare furiously out of the window, determined not to let the tears that I can feel behind my eyes spill down my face. If she's not going to cry then neither am I. Perhaps we haven't given her enough to fight for – maybe we have to show her it's worth giving it everything she's got to stay here with us.

Mum and Dad are having a quiet conversation now and I zone out, envying Isaac with his iPod. After a while Dad says that we have to leave if we're to be home in time for tea – Isaac finds it really hard if mealtimes are later than normal.

I'm feeling really mad at Mum and I don't want to stay here any longer so I head straight to the door. Isaac follows me while Dad gives her a hug, and then we all step into the corridor and Dad closes her door. Suddenly I feel guilty for leaving – it's so confusing, I just can't figure out how I'm feeling from one second to the next at the moment.

'Go on ahead, Dad – I'll catch you up,' I tell him and watch for a moment as he and Isaac head down the corridor. Then I turn back and open the door again. Mum is slumped in her chair, eyes closed and looking totally exhausted. Her face is drained and pale and her body looks as if nothing is holding it up – she reminds me of a puppet I used to play with after its strings tangled, that ended up flopped in the corner of my toy box, limp and useless.

'Bye, Mum,' I whisper, but she doesn't even open her eyes to look at me.

I close the door as quietly as I can and start walking back towards the stairs. By the time I've caught up with Dad and Isaac outside I am feeling more tired than I can ever remember being. I don't even have the energy to argue with Isaac about who sits in the front of the car, and sink on to the back seat, glad of the peace and quiet.

As we drive through town I think about Mum, all on her own, knowing what is going to happen to her but not knowing what it'll feel like or even when it'll happen. I wonder if she might feel a bit like I did on Transition Day to high school. That weird feeling of not really belonging anywhere. I'd been at Compton Heath Primary for seven years and I thought that the hardest part would be when we left, but actually it wasn't. The most difficult time was after Transition Day when we'd visited high school but had to go back to Compton Heath for a few weeks. It just felt wrong – like my time there was done and I was an impostor. Everything was so familiar but really strange at the same time. The chairs were too small and the rooms felt shabby and the teachers suddenly seemed different. It felt like losing something that belonged to me – and then realizing it was never really mine in the first place.

Then I think that this is a stupid comparison to make cos I had a visit to high school and got to see the changing rooms in the PE department, and the canteen and the science labs – but Mum only gets to visit where she is going once, and then she has to stay there. No Transition Day for her, no chance to get ready or to learn about all the new rules.

Maybe that's the whole point of St Mary's Hospice, I think – to prepare her for what's going to happen. Although I don't really see how anyone can do that when nobody can agree on exactly what happens when you die.

We've reached home now and Dad pulls up on our driveway. He turns the engine off and we all sit in silence for a minute, listening to that ticking sound the engine makes as it cools down. I look at our house. It's not dark outside yet, but it looks dark inside. The windows seem to stare emptily on to the street, and I know that even when we're inside with every light turned on, and the radio blaring in the kitchen, or when Leah comes over after work to check that we're OK it'll still feel bleak and lonely.

I wonder if I've missed the real reason why Mum is staying at St Mary's instead of wanting to spend every waking moment with us. Maybe it isn't to prepare *her* for when she's not here – maybe it's to help us get ready? Maybe she thinks we need to get used to a home without her in it. Perhaps she reckons that Dad needs time to work out how to use the washing machine – if that's the case, then her plan is failing miserably cos I haven't had any clean socks for days now.

It wouldn't surprise me if, even now, my mum is trying to do the right thing for the rest of us. The thing is – she's got it horribly wrong this time. This can't possibly be the best thing for our family. Sure, I thought it was difficult when she was really ill at home last week, but I was stupid and I didn't know it'd be even harder when she wasn't here with us. And that place – it's just letting her give up. If she was at home we could show her, all the time, that she's tougher than this thing – that she can fight and duck and dive and beat it, for us.

And there, on the back seat of our car, I make a decision. 'I'm not going to visit Mum again,' I whisper. I know this is the right thing to do – but my throat suddenly feels dry and my voice comes out all croaky.

'What?' says Dad, half turning in the driver's seat to take a better look at me.

'I'm not going back to that place,' I say again, sounding a bit more confident this time.

'Oh, Liv.' Dad sighs and runs his fingers through his hair. He needs a haircut – I can't believe Mum didn't have a go at him about it today. She'd never normally let him leave it this long – he looks a state. 'I know it's hard seeing her there but –'

'No! I'm not going. If she wants to see me so much then she can come home. To our house. Where we all live.'

'It's just not that simple, Liv.'

'It *is*. It should be, anyway.'

'But there're things she needs – things we – I – can't give her at home.' Dad has turned away, his back to me now, and is staring out of the front window.

I can't believe he's being as passive as Mum – both allowing all of our lives to be ruined. What's wrong with them? Why won't they actually *do* something?

'Do you *want* her to stay there?' I yell at him. I don't mean to shout at him but it isn't fair – it just isn't.

'No!' Dad whips his head round to look at me again and he sounds shocked. 'I want her home, just like you do!'

'So whose idea was it to send her away?' I ask. Dad doesn't say anything and I feel bad pushing him like this, but I really need his help to get Mum to see sense and come home. By now Isaac has taken his earphones out and I can hear tinny music coming from his abandoned iPod. He's looking interested so I decide to enlist his help.

'Dad? Did you send Mum to that place?'

'No, Liv, I didn't.' Dad is looking at me carefully and I can see dark rings round his eyes. 'I wanted Mum to stay at home but she thought it'd be better – easier – for everyone if she went to St Mary's.'

'Well, she was wrong,' I say, turning to Isaac. 'Do *you* want Mum at home?'

Isaac looks from me to Dad and thinks about what I've asked him. For a moment the only sounds in the car come from his earphones and my breathing – I sound like I've just run up a hill. I try to calm down and wait for Isaac, crossing my fingers behind my back and willing him to say the right thing for once.

'It would be good if Mum was at home,' he begins and I feel my fingers start to unfurl. 'Mum should be here, where she belongs. Dad forgot to dry out my trainers after my games lesson yesterday and I think I might have contracted trench foot.'

Dad snorts back a laugh and rubs Isaac's arm as the tension in the car disappears. Then he catches my eye and smiles at me. I've said enough for now – I need to give Operation Bring Mum Home time to develop, but I'm confident that I've planted the seeds in Dad's mind and I know I can trust him to work on Mum. I mean it, though, I think to myself as I get out of the car – I have vowed never to set foot in St Mary's Hospice again, as long as I may live.

Tuesday

And now everything is happening very quickly. Dad went to see Mum without me and Isaac, and then last night he brought Mum home from St Mary's. Instead of going to bed, she came to sit at the kitchen table and told us all – Dad, Leah, Isaac and me – that she wouldn't go back to the hospice or the hospital again. She had wasted enough time and now she wanted to be here with us.

'Hurray!' said Isaac, immediately getting up to put a smiley face on the wall planner – his way of telling us that he's having a good day. 'Aunt Leah cooked pasta for tea yesterday, but it wasn't the right sort. We need you here, Mum.'

As soon as I wake, I go out to the studio and grab my camera. I know exactly what I want to take photographs of now and it feels good to have a mission, something to be focusing on. These are the most important pictures I'll ever take – proof that my mum is the bravest, strongest, best mum in the world.

I stay off school again today. I don't even think about going and Mum and Dad don't say a word. I help Leah sort out Isaac's packed lunch and remind him that he needs his (now dry) trainers, and then I wave him off in the taxi. But after that I just go upstairs and sit down on a chair next to Mum. She's asleep so I take a photo of her and then read my book, but when she wakes up I know that she's glad I'm there.

This afternoon, a nurse comes to check up on Mum and give her some medicine. Dad tells me to nip to the corner shop for some teabags and milk while she talks to him. I haven't been there since Isaac's meltdown a couple of months ago and it seems weird – the shop is exactly the same yet my life has changed beyond recognition.

When I return I go back upstairs to give Mum the Mars bar I've bought her as a little treat. She's properly awake now and sitting up in bed, propped up on lots of pillows. She asks me to open the curtains as wide as they'll go.

'We need to let the air in, Liv. Open the window

too,' she says. 'Let me feel that gorgeous summer breeze on my arms!'

I do as she asks and then sit down on the side of her bed.

'Are you OK, Mum?' I ask her. 'Do you need me to get painkillers or something?'

'That lovely nurse has given me everything I need, sweetheart. Try not to worry,' she tells me.

I look away, out of the window, so that she won't see my tears. 'How can I *not* worry?' I mutter.

Mum gently turns my face towards her. 'I'm OK, Liv. And I can be OK because I know that *you'll* be OK. And Dad. And Isaac.'

'Aren't you sad?' I ask her.

'Of course I am, and I'm angry. I never imagined that I wouldn't see my beautiful children grow up. But I'm starting to realize that I'm lucky too – because I've had all this time with you already and that's better than having nothing at all.'

'But –' I start, and she just carries on.

'I might never have met your dad and then I wouldn't have had the joy of knowing you and Isaac. I wouldn't have seen Isaac grow into a young man who works *so* hard every day that it humbles me and makes me realize how easy my life is. I wouldn't have had the honour of watching you become a confident, caring young woman who makes me laugh more than she will ever know. I didn't *have* to have any of these experiences but I was lucky because I did have them. And I know that I've helped give you both the start you needed – now it's time for you to spread your wings and get ready for a solo flight.'

'I don't think we're ready,' I say, starting to cry.

'Oh, my darling, we never think we'll be ready,' says Mum, holding me tightly, her voice sounding croaky and strange. 'If I'd lived to a hundred and two I'd never have felt prepared to let you go. But life is ready for you, Liv – and I *know* you are capable of living your life as loudly as you can.'

We hug each other for a while longer, both crying a little, and then Dad comes in.

'What's that window doing open?' he exclaims.

'I wanted it open,' Mum tells him, reaching for a tissue and wiping her eyes.

'Honestly, Rachel, you'll catch your death of cold!' he says.

Mum raises one eyebrow at him, very slowly. 'I don't think that's much of a concern, do you?' she drawls and starts laughing.

Dad looks at her and smiles. 'You're a terrible patient,' he tells her.

'I know, I know – I'm demanding and bossy and ungrateful,' she says, and they both laugh again.

If someone had told me, a few weeks ago, what my family would be going through, and asked me to describe the mood in our house, I would never have known that laughter and fun and silly jokes would be such a big part of our days.

'Liv – are the primroses still out in the back garden?' asks Mum.

'Yeah, I saw some the other day. There's actually a few left that haven't been trampled by Isaac and his football too!'

Mum lies back on the pillows. 'I'd love to see them,' she tells Dad.

'I'm not sure –' he begins but she interrupts him.

'No, don't worry, Dan, I'm not saying I want to go outside. Crikey – getting downstairs feels like an expedition to Everest at the moment! No – it's just that I've always loved this time of year, when you can feel summer waiting round the corner. I don't want to miss my last spring, that's all.'

'Don't say stuff like that, Mum,' I say firmly. 'By next spring you might be better, up and about on your feet and doing the garden yourself.'

'Liv –' whispers Mum, but I don't want to have this conversation with her again.

'Positive thinking, Mum – remember? That book I borrowed from the library said that the human mind is capable of amazing things and we can make anything happen if we want it really badly, and try very hard.'

'I know, Liv – but sometimes we need to face facts, even if we don't like them.'

Mum looks sad again now and really tired. Dad tucks her covers in a bit tighter and beckons me out of the room and we tiptoe downstairs. I start to head into the living room where Leah is vacuuming, but Dad stops me.

'Actually, Liv, I've got an idea. Something to cheer Mum up, and I need your help.'

And then he tells me the best idea I've heard in weeks and I get to work.

Wednesday

I've been outside since six o'clock this morning. I was so excited about Dad's idea that I couldn't sleep and I'm sure that it's going to help Mum to start fighting back. At half past seven Isaac appears at the back door, looking out at me in confusion.

'Liv – what are you doing?'

'I'm digging up primroses and putting them into pots!' I tell him, standing up straight and stretching out. This gardening stuff is actually quite hard work.

'Why can't you leave them where they are?' Isaac asks.

'Well, Mum really wants to sit in the garden only she can't because she's too poorly – so we're going to take the garden in to her!' I say. 'We can put the pots in her bedroom and as soon as the garden centre opens, Dad's going to buy a little tree – she'll love it and it will remind her how fab it is to be outdoors, so she'll want to get better. Then she can be in the garden for real!'

Isaac doesn't say anything and I can tell he's thinking about what I've said. I carry on potting the plants and after a few minutes I sense him stepping outside and coming to stand beside me on the lawn. I look down and see his bare feet on the grass, toes scrunching up at the cold, damp sensation, and I stare at him in amazement. Isaac cannot bear certain sensations and I have never, in my whole life, seen him go barefoot outdoors – not in the garden, not even on the beach.

'Let me help?' he asks me, and puts his hand out for a trowel. Wordlessly, I pass it to him and watch as he makes a small hole in the pot of dirt that I've found. Another first – *I can't wait to tell Mum*, I think to myself.

We keep going until all the pots I've found are filled with the last of the primroses and daffodils. I line them all up on the patio and we step back, proud of our efforts. I'm sure this will help Mum see that she needs to make sure she's still here next spring.

'Mum's really ill, isn't she.' It's not a question and

when I turn to Isaac he refuses to meet my eye, looking down at the paving stones and scuffing his toes against the rough edges.

'Yeah, she is,' I tell him.

'What will we do when she's dead?' Isaac asks.

I suck in my breath and try not to show him how shocked I am to hear those words. It sounds so harsh, hearing him just say it like that. I think about what to tell him. I want to yell at him for not having positive thoughts and I'm scared that him saying it out loud might be bad karma or something – but I can't say that. And deep down inside, I'm not entirely sure that thinking positively is going to be enough here. There's no point in lying but I don't know how to make this OK for him. Because it really isn't OK.

I tell the truth. 'I don't know, Isaac.'

'Will we forget about her?'

'No!' I cry. 'We definitely won't forget about her! How could we? She's always going to be our mum.'

'I'm scared, Liv,' he says quietly. 'I'm not good at remembering things. I forget stuff all the time.'

'But this is different – it's really important!'

'But I forget important stuff too. I forgot to feed Harold – and he died.'

Harold the goldfish was Mum and Dad's one attempt at giving Isaac responsibility for a pet. It was not a success.

'Yes, but, Isaac – Harold didn't die because you forgot to feed him. He died because you thought he might like a day out and put him in your pocket!' Mum and Dad had taken us to an aquarium and didn't know that Isaac had brought Harold along until he took him out of his coat pocket and held him up to 'show him his fishy friends'.

I take hold of Isaac's hand. 'I promise you that I won't let you forget about Mum,' I tell him. 'Now come on – you're going to be late for your taxi if we don't get a move on.'

'What time is it, Liv?' asks Isaac.

I glance at my watch. 'Just gone eight o'clock and you haven't had breakfast yet, so hurry up!'

I start towards the back door but Isaac isn't moving. I look back at him and grab his hand, giving it a yank. 'Come on, Isaac!'

'No, Liv. What *time* is it?'

I huff, feeling exasperated. Now is not a good moment for Isaac to get weird on me. 'I already told you. But if you want the *exact* time, then it's now four minutes past eight. Satisfied?'

'No! Liv – just do the time thing!' Isaac is starting to get frustrated and I am about to leave him in the garden and find Dad so that he can deal with this, when I see what Isaac is holding in his other hand. A dandelion with a head full of seeds.

And suddenly I understand. I remember a few summers ago when Mum showed me and Isaac how to blow dandelions so we could tell the time. I got bored well before he did – and he really drove me crazy making me blow those dandelion heads, one after the other. Every now and then we'd actually get the real time on the dandelion clock and Isaac would burst out laughing – a sound that we don't hear very often.

Gently, I take the dandelion from Isaac. 'Get ready to count,' I warn him, 'because this is a once-only event.' And then I start blowing.

'One o'clock!' chants Isaac. The dandelion seeds flutter a few feet and then fall to the ground.

'Two o'clock! Three o'clock!'

Just as he says 'Four o'clock', a breeze gusts across the patio and takes the rest of the seeds. We watch them float through the air and across the garden.

'Right. It's four o'clock,' I say, throwing the

bald dandelion stem on to the grass. '*Now* will you get ready for school?'

Isaac lets me lead him through the back door and into the kitchen, and I'm sure he's remembering happier days when life seemed simple and the passing of time could be told by dandelion clocks, and nothing else mattered.

Later, when Isaac has gone to school, Dad takes me to the garden centre and we choose a gorgeous little tree in a pot. We bring it home and tie ribbons around the branches and then, when Leah comes down to tell us that Mum's fast asleep, we all leap into action. We carry up the pots and put them on her dressing table and bedside table, and some on top of the wardrobe. Dad puts the tree in the corner of the room where she can see it, even when she's lying down. I bring up one extra flowerpot that I planted all on my own, after Isaac had left for school. It's not as big as the others, but I think it's beautiful and that it might make Mum laugh. And then we creep out of the room and wait for her to wake up.

We're sitting round the kitchen table when we hear a cry from upstairs. I stand up and run, Dad just in front of me and Leah behind. My heart is racing – what if something's wrong with Mum? We burst into the room and look at the bed. Mum is sitting up, smiling and laughing and pointing at the room we've made for her.

'You did all this? For me?' she cries.

I race round to the side of her bed and hug her.

'I *love* it! It really feels like summer is on its way, at long last. Thank you, thank you – it's fantastic!'

'Does it feel a bit like being outside?' I ask her.

'It's even better,' she says. 'I can be all cosy in bed *and* be part of the garden too.' She looks over at Dad. 'I love the tree,' she tells him. 'It's just like –'

'The ones we had when we got married!' Dad finishes for her. 'I know you think I didn't pay any attention to our wedding plans, but I do remember the trees – and the incredibly gorgeous bride!'

'It must have taken all of you ages,' Mum says. I tell her that Isaac helped, and describe him walking on the grass with bare feet and getting muddy hands. Mum looks teary-eyed. 'That makes it even more special,' she says.

We all sit on the bed and chat for a while, not talking about anything important, just everyday things. It's nice in Mum's room with the sun streaming through the window – I fetch my camera and take lots of pictures of her, some of her leaning back against Dad and a few of her pretending to eat the Mars bar I bought her yesterday. She says she doesn't really have much of an appetite, but it's funny watching her messing about, pulling silly faces. My favourite photo, though, is one of her on her own, surrounded by all our flowers and smiling at me in a way that makes me feel good inside. After a while, Dad says that Mum needs her rest, so we all stand to leave her for a snooze. Just as I'm about to go, she calls me back and whispers in my ear.

'Those flowers over there,' she says, pointing to the special, funny little pot I'd placed on the table by the window. 'They're my favourite. I can't ever walk past one of those without wanting to pick it and blow all the seeds off! And when they've got their flowers they remind me that beautiful things can happen, even when you least expect it. They look so gorgeous, all mixed up together – I've never seen a plant pot like it!' She pulls me to her and kisses me on my forehead. 'I love you so much, Olivia. Thank you for letting me get to know you. You and Isaac have made me the luckiest woman in the whole wide world.' She lies back on the pillows. 'Will you do me a favour, sweetheart? Put that pot over here, right next to the bed where I can always see it.'

I move the pot carefully on to her bedside table and then bend down and give her a hug. She closes her eyes and I start to sing a bit of the lullaby that she used to sing to me. I'm a rubbish singer, though, and I can't remember the words properly so I hum most of it, just singing the last two lines.

'Lay thee down now and rest,
May thy slumber be blessed.'

Maybe I'm not as awful a singer as I thought cos by the time I'm finished Mum is fast asleep.

'Sweet dreams, Mum,' I tell her. 'I love you too.' And then I leave her in peace.

I'm sitting in my room now, by the window. The house feels strangely empty. Isaac came home a few hours ago and we all had tea, although nobody was very hungry. Leah tried to get us to play a game of cards, but we were all distracted and Isaac ended up getting cross because we weren't keeping to the proper rules, so we gave up and I decided to go and read a book.

I can't settle on anything, though. I know I have loads of homework to do but that seems so unimportant right now. I could print the photos that I took today, but I'd have to go outside to the studio and that feels like too much effort.

That's why I'm sitting here, just listening to the sounds of the house. I can hear the faint sound of the television coming from downstairs and I know that Leah and Isaac are watching some silly quiz show. I could go and watch it with them but it doesn't really seem fair if we're all together down there while Mum's on her own up here.

Mum's diaries are on my bedside table – I've got through loads of entries. She's been revising for some exams, although, from the sound of it, she's spent longer colour-coding her revision timetable than actually doing any work. I read something last night that I just can't stop thinking about so I grab her diary and turn to 23 June 1989.

I'm going to try to write more often in this diary to record this crucial time in my life. Maybe I'll use it for future reference. Who knows, one day I might have a husband and kids (!) and I might let them read it! How mega-embarrassing! I hope I'll be a brilliant mum, though - I'll always try to understand how my kids are feeling and I'll be on exactly the same wavelength as them. I don't understand it when adults forget what it's really like to be a kid - surely it can't be THAT hard to remember? I'm gonna let my kids do whatever they want - I'll trust them to make their own decisions. I'm gonna be more like their best friend than their mum - then we'll all be happy!!

Actually, I'll probably burn these diaries before I get too old. Imagine if they fell into the wrong hands! I'll just have to tell my kids how amazing and brilliant I was when I was a teenager.

I am so glad that Mum didn't burn her diaries and I'm really happy that she hasn't actually tried to be my best friend. I don't need any more friends – I just need my mum.

I hear Dad clattering around in the kitchen, loading the dishwasher, and then his footsteps coming upstairs and going into his and Mum's room. It's funny how reassuring these noises are and how I can picture what's going on in each room of the house just by listening.

Now there's the sound of the noisy kettle going on in the kitchen – there must be an ad break. Leah will be making two cups of that disgusting chamomile tea that she makes every night and brings up to Mum. She swears that it's healthy, but I can't see how anything that smells so bad can do you any good. I can hear Isaac channel-hopping on the television – he has a few adverts that he really loves and every time there's an ad break he switches channels as quickly as possible, hoping to find his favourite ones. If there were a channel that only had adverts, then Isaac would be really happy.

Mum's bedroom door opens and then closes gently and I listen for Dad's footsteps, expecting them to head back downstairs. Instead, everything is quiet. I picture Dad standing on the landing outside their room, and I'm just about to get up to look when I hear him moving and then he opens my door.

Suddenly I can't hear the hysterical laughter from the studio audience on the television. The kettle must have boiled because I can't hear that either. All I can hear is the sound of Dad, telling me that Mum has gone. That lying in her bed, listening to the sounds of her home, she has left us and she won't be coming back.

I get up slowly and go out into the hall. I stand outside her bedroom door, very still. I don't need to go inside to see her – instead I just listen. And as I listen, I'm certain that I can hear the evening breeze, coming through the open window and whispering through the room, gently blowing the seeds from the flowers in Mum's pot across her bed, marking the time that she closed her eyes for the last time ever. I imagine her, drifting quietly away, looking at the flowers I planted so carefully this morning and that she told me made her happy. And I am glad that my dandelion clocks were the last thing that she looked at before she went.

Friday

There are lots of things that need to be organized when someone dies. It's amazing really, how much has to be sorted out. Not that I've got anything to do with that. Dad is really busy, on the phone constantly, telling people what's happened and trying to find out when we can have the funeral. Apparently it'll be really soon, which seems weird because we won't have had time to get used to the idea that Mum's not here before we have to say goodbye to her.

Dad told Isaac last night after he'd told me. Leah cried a lot and spent ages in Mum's room, talking to her. Dad asked if we wanted to see Mum. I didn't want to, but Dad thought it might help Isaac to understand that Mum was gone. Isaac went into Mum's room with Dad but came back out straight away. He got a bit cross and said he didn't know who that was in Mum's bed, but it wasn't Mum, and could Dad please make whoever it was go away. He didn't cry or anything, but when I went into his room later on he was just lying on his bed, looking at the ceiling. His PlayStation wasn't even turned on.

Alice called me this afternoon. Her mum must have spoken to Dad because she already knew. It wasn't very easy to talk to her – I think she was scared about saying the wrong thing and I didn't have the energy to think about other stuff to talk about.

People keep asking me how I am but I can't answer them. Not because I don't want to but because I just don't know. It all seems so unreal. I didn't think it was supposed to happen like this. On television, they always have loads of time to say goodbye when someone dies and it's always really sad but kind of lovely too. This just seems too quick – I actually feel a bit embarrassed, like we got it wrong somehow. Dad tried to explain to me that we have no control over stuff like this and just have to deal with what gets thrown at us. That sounds rubbish. I want to choose what happens to me. Mum's always said there's no such thing as fate – that we decide what happens to us.

If it's true, then that means she decided to leave me. I just don't know what to think any more.

I've come down to the kitchen for a drink, but now I'm here I can't seem to find the energy even to take the juice out of the fridge. I sit down at the kitchen table and wonder why the house feels different. Like something is missing. Then I realize there *is* something missing – *someone* missing – and it hits me that nothing will ever be the same again. It might look the same – same fridge, same table, same brand of juice that Mum always chooses. But it can't be the same, not really.

I sit in the kitchen for ages until it starts to get dark. I should turn on the light or put the lamp on, make it cosy like Mum does, but I can't be bothered. I'm just starting to wonder if it's possible to stay in this chair all night when I hear someone thundering down the stairs and then the kitchen door bursts open and the light blazes on.

'It's dark,' says Isaac. I try to hide the tears that seem to have been flowing down my face for hours, but they just keep on coming and wiping them away doesn't seem to make a difference. Isaac walks across the room and looks at me very carefully. He looks really serious as he leans towards me and examines my face. I say nothing and watch as he straightens up and takes a few more steps until he's standing by the wall planner, looking at the photo display of faces that I made for him. Eventually he finds what he's looking for and turns round, walking back until he's standing behind me.

'You're sad,' he says.

'Yes,' I tell him and then my brother, who has never tried to work out how I'm feeling in my whole life, pats me on the shoulder. I sit very still while his hand moves awkwardly up and down, as if he's trying to remember the rules for making someone feel better.

After a while, when the patting gets too much, I reach back and grasp his hand in mine. And then we stay, holding hands, while the world outside the kitchen gets darker and darker.

Sunday

I'm in Dad's studio, printing out my pictures. The room is dark and I feel safe in here. Over the last few days our house has been full of visitors – people wanting to pay their respects to Mum (although she's not here now, she's at the funeral home waiting for tomorrow), people wanting to bring dishes of food for Dad and us, and people wanting to hug Isaac and me and tell us how sorry they are. I know they all mean well but we could do without it. Isaac is getting seriously wound up with all the changes and he shouts at anyone who attempts to touch him. Fortunately, nearly everyone knows it's a bad idea to try to hug him – although there was nearly a nasty moment when the editor of the magazine that Mum wrote for came to visit.

I take my photos over to Dad's big table and turn on the lamp. Mum smiles up at me. These are the last photos I took of her and they're my best ever. I've managed to really capture my mum and I know that these pictures will definitely make it into my box.

Dad gave me the box this morning. Isaac's got one too. Dad says it's a memory box, and that we can put whatever we want inside. We don't have to show anyone else if we don't want to – it's a box for putting anything in that reminds us of Mum. I knew instantly what I wanted to use my box for and that's why I've come to the studio. I'm choosing the photos of Mum that show me who she is and what's important to her. I just wish I had more pictures of her.

Isaac loves his box and started putting things in it straight away. I know I probably shouldn't have done, but I wanted to know how he was going to remember Mum, so I sneaked into his room while he was in the bathroom earlier and took a tiny peek. Inside his box was a sock, a bookmark, a teaspoon and a friendship bracelet that I remember making for Mum last summer. I didn't know whether to laugh or cry – but I guess, as long as it makes him feel close to Mum, it's up to him what he chooses. And I suppose it's really none of my business either.

I saw Ben this morning but he didn't see me. Dad was out in the back garden with Isaac, and Leah had gone off to the supermarket to stock up on food for tomorrow – apparently people expect food at a funeral, which I think is weird because I don't want to eat anything at the moment. I was in my room and I heard a knock on the front door, only it was really quiet, as if whoever was knocking wasn't certain they really wanted anyone to hear them. I peeped out of my window, making sure that I was hidden behind the curtain, and saw Ben, standing on the doorstep. He looked a bit scared and I couldn't work out why he was just standing there – but then he shoved something through the letterbox and ran back down our path. He jumped into a car that was waiting outside our gate with a woman inside. I guess it must have been his mum. I saw her put her arm round him and glance up at our house, so I ducked back behind the curtain and when I looked again they'd gone.

When I went downstairs there was an envelope

with my name on, lying on the doormat. It's in my room now, next to my bed. I haven't opened it and I don't think I will – but I like seeing it there and knowing that, for now, Ben hasn't forgotten me.

Monday

It was raining earlier and I thought that seemed right for today – but the sun came out while we were in the church and actually, that seems totally perfect. The road is still wet, though, and I can hear the squelching sound of the tyres as we speed back towards our house. I really like that noise – for some reason it reminds me of getting up in the middle of the night to go on holiday and falling asleep in the back of the car, wondering where we'd be when I woke up.

I wish I could fall asleep now and wake up when today is over. In fact, I quite like the idea of escaping altogether and waking up tomorrow somewhere completely different. I wonder if this would be any easier if Mum's things weren't all around us and if we were somewhere that nobody knew us. Maybe it would be worse.

We're nearly home now and I know that I have to be brave for this next bit. Dad didn't want to invite people back to our house after the funeral – he thought it'd be too much for Isaac – but Leah persuaded him. She said that lots of people cared about Mum and that they need a chance to say goodbye to her. Then she said that people want to help and that he, Dan, shouldn't be so proud. So Dad asked Mrs Green from down the road to look after Isaac. He loves going to her house – she feeds him cake and lets him mess about with her late husband's collection of model aeroplanes. I wanted to go with him (I pretended to Dad that I thought Isaac might need me, but really I was worried about seeing the grown-ups being all sad), but Dad said I should stay with him and that people would like to see me.

'Liv? We're here,' says Dad, putting his hand on my shoulder. I look up in surprise and he's right – the car has stopped outside our garden gate.

I suddenly realize how scared I am. Dad has got out of the car and is thanking the driver. I can see them both looking at me but my legs won't work and I have no idea how I'm supposed to move. Maybe I'll have to stay here forever, in the back of this long, black car that only ever carries sadness and tears.

Dad comes round to my side of the car and opens the door. He reaches in for my hand and gently pulls me.

'It's OK,' he says quietly to me. 'You've done the hard part. We can do this together.' And I feel my legs starting to move and then I'm out of the car and walking up the path, Dad's hand holding firmly on to mine.

I hope he's right. The funeral was awful. I couldn't really look at anything or listen to anyone – instead I made myself look at the stained-glass window above the altar and tried to count all the cherubim and seraphim and angels. But I don't know the difference between them, or if there even *is* a difference, so it was a pretty pointless activity. It stopped me having to look at the box lying in front of the altar, though – because I knew that if I started looking and I started thinking and remembering, then I wouldn't be able to stand there and sing 'This little light of mine' with everybody else, and as it was Mum's favourite hymn I wanted to sing it as well as I could. Mum's friend Beth was sitting in the row behind us and it took all of my efforts to ignore the sound of her crying. I know everyone is sad but I really wanted her to just shut up until she was somewhere that I didn't have to hear her. I saw Alice sitting with her mum and dad at the back of the church. I didn't tell her it was Mum's funeral today so I'm not really sure how she found out. I suppose everybody knows now – I hate the idea that people are talking about us, but it was nice of her to come.

Dad opens the front door and a wall of noise hits us. He instantly shuts it and looks down at me, with a look of surprise on his face.

'What's going on, Dad?' I ask him.

'Sounds like someone's having a party in there!' he says, starting to smile.

'Is that what we're supposed to be doing?' I say. I'm feeling confused – I thought that funerals were meant to be quiet and miserable, full of people standing around wailing and sobbing. But I can hear people talking. There's even the sound of people laughing. I look at Dad, waiting for him to tell me what to do.

'I don't think there are any rules for this situation, Liv,' says Dad, 'but I do know that your mum would have thought this was an excellent way to celebrate today.'

I'm shocked now.

'Celebrate? What are we supposed to be celebrating? There's nothing good about this but there're people in there *laughing*. What's wrong with everyone?' I turn round and run down the path at the side of our house, into the back garden. I'm furious and upset and not sure about anything any more.

I hear footsteps pounding behind and Dad catches up with me on the lawn, grabbing hold of my hand.

'We're celebrating Mum's life today. She made many people happy and had lots of friends – and they've all come here to share stories about her and to remember the happy times they've had with her. It's OK, Liv. Mum would have loved this!'

I yank my hand out of his and plonk myself down on the garden swing seat. 'Well, I'm not going inside! I don't want to celebrate. Mum doesn't think this is OK and neither do I – and I can't pretend that it is!'

'Nobody wants you to pretend anything, Livvy. And if you'd rather stay out here, then that's fine.' Dad sits down next to me on the swing. I turn and look at him.

'What are you doing?' I ask.

'Well, I don't know for certain, but I'm pretty sure your mum would be furious with me if I left you sitting here on your own,' he says.

'But all those people are in our house! You have to go and talk to them and make sure they're OK!' I'm suddenly feeling really cold and shaky, even though the sun is shining.

'Oh, I think they'll be fine without me! They've come to think about your mum and they can do that even with us sitting out here. And Leah's inside handing out cups of tea and sandwiches, so they won't starve!'

'I don't want to make you stay out here,' I tell Dad. 'I'll go inside if you want me to.'

'Liv,' Dad says. 'There is nowhere I would rather be right now than sitting here with you.'

So we sit together in the garden, swinging gently, not really speaking much, but the silence is a good silence and I think Dad is doing what I'm doing – just thinking about Mum. I curl up against Dad and he gives me his jacket to wear – it feels cosy.

Leah comes out to find us after a while, having spotted us through the kitchen window. She brings us two cups of tea and Dad asks her to explain to all the guests that he is needed elsewhere, but that he's really grateful they all came. Leah tells him that they already know that and they all totally understand.

It starts to get a bit cloudy and the lights go on inside the house. We keep swinging, watching people moving in front of the windows, and eventually I see that there is less and less movement, until the only silhouette is Leah's, washing up at the kitchen sink.

Dad gets up stiffly and stretches. 'Come on – it's freezing out here now. Let's get you in and warm before I collect Isaac from Mrs Green's.'

We walk through the back door and into the kitchen.

'Ah – that's right! Appear when I've done all the clearing up!' jokes Leah, coming over and giving me a big hug.

'Sorry,' I say, but she winks at me, letting me know that it's OK really.

'All right?' she asks Dad and he nods at her. 'Everything you asked for is on the dining-room table,' she tells him. 'And more, from what I could see!'

'That's great,' he says, and puts his arm round her. 'Thank you so much for everything you've done, Leah – we couldn't have managed without you.'

'Of course you could!' says Leah, trying to make light of his comment – but I can tell she's pleased. 'It's only what Rachel would have done for me, anyway.'

I think that is a weird thing to say and wonder what today would have been like if it was Leah who had died, and not Mum. And then I feel hot and guilty inside because I love Leah, but if I could choose between them, I would choose for Mum to stay with me, every time.

'And she would be very proud of her little sister, I know that,' Dad tells her. He turns to me. 'Right, young lady – you need a hot bath followed by a hot chocolate and then some cheese on toast. No arguments!'

I follow him upstairs and stand in the bathroom while he runs me a bath. He pours in a capful of Mr Matey bubble bath and I haven't got the heart to tell him I haven't used Mr Matey since the last time he ran me a bath – about four years ago. Anyway, he's treating me like I'm a little kid and to be honest, it feels quite nice.

When the bath is full, Dad leaves me on my

own and I get undressed and sink beneath the bubbles. I think about today and how people deal with death in different ways. While we were in the garden, Dad told me about Mexico, where everyone celebrates the Day of the Dead each year. He said they party and eat lots and laugh lots – all as a way of remembering people they love who have died. I can't imagine us doing anything like that, but I suppose it's quite a cool idea. He also told me about a Native American Indian tribe where the women cut their hair if somebody close to them dies. I definitely wouldn't like to do that. And Mum would have a *fit* if she thought I was chopping off my hair after all the months of effort it's taken to grow my fringe out. I'm pleased that Mum has so many friends who love her – but I'm also glad that Dad and I stayed outside on our own, just us, remembering Mum.

The bathwater is cooling down and my toes are going wrinkly, which I really hate, so I clamber out and get warm in my pyjamas and dressing gown. I head downstairs and can hear that Isaac is back – he's moaning at Leah for not cutting the crusts off his toast. Dad meets me at the bottom of the stairs with a mug of hot chocolate.

'Better?' he asks me and I nod. 'Good. Before

you have some food I want you to see something.'
He leads me into the dining room and up to the
table.

I look down, unable to process what I'm seeing.
'What? How–?' I stutter, not sure what I'm
looking at.

Dad seems pleased with my reaction. 'All those
people who were here today? They all knew Mum
in different ways. They all shared times with her
that they thought you'd like to know about – so I
asked each of them to bring one memory with them,
just for you. And here they all are!'

Spread out on the table are lots and lots of
pictures. And Mum is in every single one of them.
I step forward and pick one up. A very young-
looking Mum is eating a huge ice cream and
pointing at the Eiffel Tower, a big grin on her face.
I put it down and choose another – Mum in a
rowing boat. I start to pick them up as quickly as I
can, hungry for more memories. Mum in a beautiful
floaty dress that I've not seen before, Mum on a
motorbike (she'd always said her most important
rule was that I *never* go on a motorbike!), Mum
sitting cross-legged on some grass making a long
daisy chain. This last one makes me smile – I'd
forgotten what an expert daisy-chain maker she's

always been. I look at photo after photo of Mum, some of her on her own, some of her with friends, and quite a few of her and Dad, holding each other and smiling at the camera.

'I didn't have enough of my own,' I tell Dad, thinking about the photos I've taken over the last few weeks.

'We can never have enough memories, sweetheart,' he tells me, looking away from me with a weird, scrunched-up expression on his face.

Four Weeks After

I'm lying in bed, trying not to think. I'm not sure how long I've been awake but it gets light so early at the moment and once I've woken up it's really hard to go back to sleep. I never close my curtains any more and I always keep my window open, even though Isaac keeps moaning at me – he reckons it's cold. I don't bother to tell him that the cold feeling in our house has got nothing to do with my window being open. Dad mutters under his breath that I'd better start closing the window when autumn arrives or the cost of heating will bankrupt him. I don't listen, though – having my window open makes me feel closer to Mum.

'Liv! Isaac!'

I can hear Dad calling and I bury my head deeper under my duvet. My door rattles a bit as Isaac thunders past and races down the stairs to where Dad is waiting. He has a meeting with Isaac's teacher this morning and told us last night that he'd take us both to school in the car today.

I, however, have absolutely no intention of going to school. I've come a long way since my first rubbish attempt at skiving all those months ago. I am now Queen Of Bunking Off. My success is mostly based on keeping under the radar – I still go to school a couple of times a week but I rotate the days I miss so that no individual teacher senses a pattern in my absences. My school has a two-week rolling timetable so I reckon I can get away with it for quite a while yet.

'LIV!' Dad is opening the front door and I can picture him looking anxiously at the clock in the hall.

'Have you seen Liv this morning?' I hear him ask Isaac.

'No.' Isaac sounds keen to go. 'Come *on*, Dad, or we'll be late.'

'She must have gone in early. I hope she took some lunch money.' Dad sounds a bit worried and I feel a pang of guilt. For a second I'm tempted to call his name. I know that he'd be up here in an instant. He'd ask me why I'm still in bed and I could tell him everything – that some mornings it seems like my whole body is made of concrete and the prospect of getting up, dressing and leaving the house seems impossible. Maybe he'd cancel his meeting and we could all stay at home in our pyjamas, cuddled up in front of the TV, eating toast and peanut butter.

Then I hear the front door slam and I'm all alone in the empty house. I'm too late and the chance to ask Dad for a hug has gone.

I'm not really sure why I haven't gone into school today. I do know that it feels like a lonely place to be. When I went back after it happened everyone went out of their way to be nice to me. I didn't really like that cos it felt wrong – I just wanted to get on with normal stuff. But it was worse whenever anyone mentioned the word 'mum'. Everyone would freeze and then the person who'd said it would say, 'Oh sorry, Liv, really sorry – didn't mean to upset you or anything.' Like, come *on*. I'm not stupid – I know that there are mums out there, going to work, making the tea, forgetting that you need your PE kit washed by tomorrow. Just not my mum.

To be honest, it's not really any better staying at home. It's weird. All of our stuff is here, the stuff we've had forever – but it just doesn't feel like home any more. It's a bit like when you've been away on holiday and everything feels a bit different when you get home. Except that things usually go back to normal pretty quickly and I don't think our house will ever feel the same again.

I must have dozed off for a bit cos I've just looked at the clock and it's 11.30 a.m. My tummy is rumbling but I can't be bothered to think about food. It seems utterly pointless to put any effort into making a meal when it's only me that'll be eating it. I get out of bed and drag myself across the room to the door. I brace myself and open it slowly – I hate being in the house when there's nobody else here.

The house is silent. Too silent. I can hear the hall clock ticking and the sound of blood rushing in my ears – when I swallow it sounds stupidly loud. I'm wondering why I didn't just go to school where I could get lost in all the noise. If I was still friends with Alice I suppose I could have hung around with her, but since it happened I've gone out of my way to avoid her. I feel bad, like I've abandoned her, but when it first happened I didn't have the energy to deal with anyone else's sadness.

Alice phoned me up after the funeral but she just cried down the telephone and I didn't know what to say. It felt like I should be making her feel better, but she's still got *her* mum – she's got nothing to cry about.

After a few weeks I kind of understood why she was sad. I wished that I could tell her how it felt and let her try to make me feel better. But then I realized nothing could ever make me feel better and it seemed wrong even to think of being anything but sad – like being disloyal to Mum. Now I can't be near Alice in case she reminds me and makes me feel even worse. She knows everything about me and if there's anyone who could open the box in my head that I've padlocked shut, it's her – so I've just kept out of her way. It seems safer like that. I'm still here so it's obviously possible to live when your whole, entire life has been destroyed. I just have to do this my way, and that means not letting other people bring their memories and thoughts and sadness into my world.

I close the door again, walk across to my dressing table and sit down. The face staring back at me from the mirror is pale and ugly – I've got spots all across my nose. After Mum's make-up lesson I was really taking care of my skin but that was ages ago now. I ran out of cleanser early on – I know Dad would buy me some more if I ask him but I can't be bothered. I pick up my hairbrush and try to tame my mad hair. But there're so many tangles that I do what I always do and grab a scrunchie. At least when it's tied up nobody can see what a mess it is. Then I lean forward and really look at myself, right in the eyes. I'm not sure what I'm hoping to see but whatever it is, I don't find it cos there's nothing there. It's like looking at a painting on a wall – not that anyone would want to do a painting of me. The person staring back at me doesn't even begin to remind me of me.

I slump back down across my bed and stare at the ceiling. I seem to spend most of my time lying here – I'm just too tired to do much of anything else. Sometimes I sleep, which is good because it helps to kill a few more pointless hours. The only problem with sleeping is the waking. Every time I sleep, I dream – vivid, lifelike dreams that wake me up feeling, for just a second, that everything is OK. I wake up unsure about where the dream ends and reality starts, and that moment is full of joy. Then I remember.

So mostly I try not to sleep. Mostly I lie on this

bed and wonder why. I wonder if this was always going to happen – if my destiny was decided long before I knew anything about it. It makes me feel as if all the happy times were just a joke – the warm-up act before the main event. Maybe it would've been better if Mum had never been here in the first place? Perhaps this is so hard because I know what life was like before, and everywhere I look there's about a million reminders of what we used to have – of the family that we used to be. I wonder, for the thousandth time, why this had to happen to me. And the nasty, nagging voice in my head whispers that maybe, Mum just didn't love me enough to stay.

I would rather feel nothing for the rest of my life than feel like I wasn't good enough to keep her.

Five Weeks
After

The sound of the door slamming jerks me awake. I'm lying on my bed and my whole body feels stiff. I have no idea how long I've been asleep. Before I have time to sit up, I hear loud footsteps running up the stairs two at a time, and then my door crashes open so hard that it slams into the wall.

'Liv! Thank goodness you're here! What the hell are you playing at?'

I look up and see Dad staring down at me. His face is red and his eyes are full of worry.

'I was so scared, Liv. Don't *ever* do that to me again.' He rubs his face with his hands and takes a deep breath, blowing the air out in one long stream. 'I didn't know what to think. I didn't even know where you were.'

Even though my brain feels all foggy, I know why he's mad and I wonder how I've been rumbled.

I pushed it too far with the bunking off and now I've been caught. Not that I feel upset. I don't feel anything really. Dad's still talking and it's a shame that he was worried, but maybe he should have realized what was going on. I mean, he's the grown-up and meant to be in charge of everything. Mum wouldn't have fallen for my tricks – there's no chance I'd have got away with skiving school if she'd been here.

'How did you find out?' I ask. My voice sounds like it's coming from a long way away. I'm really not interested, but Dad's gone quiet and I think he's expecting me to say something.

'School rang me – said they were worried because you've missed so many days lately,' Dad answers, but he sounds distracted. He's looking at me in a really odd way and it's starting to freak me out a bit.

'What's going on, Liv? Talk to me,' he says quietly.

'I just couldn't face school today, Dad,' I tell him.

'Have you been in your room all day?' he asks, his voice sounding totally weird.

'Yeah. I've been asleep pretty much the whole time. Why – what time is it now?'

Dad doesn't answer. His face looks worried

and sad and something else that I can't quite figure out.

'Liv –' he starts and then stops. It's as if he doesn't know what to say and I don't like it.

'I'm sorry, Dad – I'll go to school tomorrow,' I say in a rush. I want him to stop looking at me like that. It's making me feel frightened.

'Why did you do it?' Dad says, and I realize that he sounds scared.

'I don't know, but I promise I won't skive again. I mean it.' Dad frowns and steps back from the bed. I sit up and swing my feet down on to the floor.

'That's not what I'm talking about, Olivia.' Dad's voice is gentle, like he's talking to a small child. 'Why did you do *that*?' He swings his arm towards my bed and I look where he's pointing.

I don't understand what I'm seeing for a moment. The bed's a state – lots of bits of paper all over the duvet, and lying on top of my pillow are Mum's sharp scissors that she used to cut Isaac and Dad's hair. I gape at the mess – how did all that get there? The paper seems familiar and I look a bit closer. My brain is struggling to make sense of what I can see and when I work it out, I wish that I hadn't.

All over the bed are photographs. They've been chopped up into different-sized pieces – they are barely recognizable. Some of them have rough edges, as if whoever did this got fed up with using scissors and started ripping them up. It looks horrible – almost like the scene of a crime. My hand reaches out and picks up one of the pieces even though my brain is screaming at it to stop. I try to close my eyes so that I don't have to look, but my body seems to have taken over and I can't control my movements.

I look at the destroyed photograph in my hand. I can see a bedside table and part of a bed. I instantly know where it was taken – I've been climbing into that bed since I first managed to escape my cot when I was a toddler. I can see an arm, a shoulder and half a face. I stifle a sob and look quickly down at the rest of the pieces scattered over my bed, searching desperately for the other half of the picture. I haven't got time to look at Dad, but I sense him coming closer and as I find the piece I'm looking for, I feel his hand on my shoulder. I grab both halves of the photograph and hold them together in front of me – and there she is. Mum, in bed, on the day that we made the indoor garden. The day that she left me. The photo has been torn right down the middle of Mum. I ram the pieces together, but it has been ripped with so much force that it won't match up properly and Mum's face is distorted. She was smiling at me when I took the picture, but now her face looks wrong. Mum is spoilt.

Holding the two halves carefully, I stare down at the floor, unable to take in any more. My mind is working overtime. What has actually happened here? Did I do this? Why would I ruin a photograph of my mum? I'm scared to look properly at the other pieces on the bed – what else has been destroyed?

'Liv?' Dad's voice is quiet and some part of my mind registers that he isn't cross with me. 'Liv, please, sweetheart – look at me.' He sits down next to me on the bed and wraps his arm round me. 'It's OK, Liv – it's all going to be OK. But you need to talk to me – tell me what's going on with you. Tell me what happened here.'

'I can't, Dad,' I whisper.

I feel Dad stiffen and then he pulls me in even closer, holding me so tightly that I can hardly breathe.

'Oh, Livvy. I know I'm not as good as your mum and I know I keep getting it wrong – but

I am trying, sweetheart, and I need you to let me in. I don't know what else to say to you.' His face is pressed against the top of my head and his voice is muffled by my hair, but I can still hear his worry and it makes me feel even worse than I already do.

'No, Dad – I mean I don't know what happened.' I pull away from him and stand up so that I can see him properly. 'You woke me up when you came into my room. I don't remember doing any of this. Maybe I didn't do it.'

And for a brief, beautiful second, I believe myself. I would actually prefer to think that some lunatic sneaked into my room while I was sleeping and cut up photographs and scattered them all over my bed. My heart lifts, for just a moment, as I wonder what sort of person would do such a terrible thing. What were the other pictures that they destroyed?

Then I catch sight of something out of the corner of my eye. I turn to look at it and solve both mysteries at once. There, on the floor, is my memory box. The lid has been thrown into a corner and the box is on its side, totally empty.

This time I can't contain my sob as I turn back to the bed and acknowledge what I knew from the start – all the photos are of Mum. The photos I've taken over the years – gone. The photos I took over her last few weeks; my project to show Mum in all her wonderfulness – gone. The photos given to me by Mum's friends after the funeral – all gone, ripped and torn and ruined. I am the sort of terrible, disgusting, evil person that would do something like this and the evidence is here, right in front of me. I don't deserve to be happy.

'I get that you're angry, Liv,' says Dad, looking at me helplessly as tears start to roll down my face.

'It's probably all my fault that she died,' I howl. 'I was just too horrible to keep her.'

'Woah – enough of that stupid talk,' says Dad, looking alarmed. 'Is that what you really think?' He stands up and grasps my shoulders, making me look at him.

I think for a moment. 'No,' I mutter. 'But there must be something wrong with me.'

'Oh, Liv – there's nothing wrong with you.' Dad sounds relieved and I can't figure out why he's not going ballistic at me.

'Err – Dad? Have you seen what I've done? There's obviously something wrong with me.' I point to the scene of the crime and start weeping again. 'I've ruined everything.'

'That's not true, Liv. Yes, OK – I agree, there is something wrong with you. Mum has died and you've done everything you can to keep it together and pretend that you're not feeling anything. Well – I'm no expert but I think that feelings need to be let out and if you don't let them, well –' he gestures towards the bed – 'then they'll find their own way of being released.'

He pulls me into another hug and I start to let myself relax a tiny bit, when I have a horrible thought.

'Mum's diaries!'

I wrench myself away from Dad and crouch down on the floor. I can see that my memory box is empty, but I can't stop myself from picking it up and shaking it and looking underneath it, just in case. They aren't there, though, so I leap up and race to the bed, where I sift through the pieces of paper, looking for anything with handwriting.

'They're not here!' I turn to Dad with relief. 'I didn't cut them up!'

He smiles at me but looks worried. I'm unsure why for a moment until it dawns on me that they're still missing. I get back on the floor and start looking under the bed.

'Look in my wardrobe, Dad,' I call to him and

am glad to hear his footsteps racing to the other side of my room. They must be in here somewhere.

We end up emptying my wardrobe, chest of drawers and bedside table, but don't find the diaries anywhere. I find some stray socks and a lot of fluff under my bed, but nothing else. We look everywhere we can think of and then we start searching the rest of the house, even though I'm sure I didn't ever leave my room.

By the time Isaac gets home we're both exhausted and miserable. Dad tries to take my mind off the diaries by telling me he'll spend the evening in his studio, printing out more photos of Mum. It won't bring back the memory pictures that her friends gave me but it'll be better than nothing, he says.

We eat tea in silence. I know that Dad is worried about me, but I'm too upset about the photos and the missing diaries to try and reassure him that I'm fine. Anyway, I don't think I am.

I wash up and listen to Isaac telling me about an experiment he did in science today. He doesn't actually need me to respond. He's not interested in what I've got to say, he just wants a captive audience, which suits me completely tonight. Dad has gone out to the studio, so when the chores are done I go upstairs – even though I've spent most of today asleep, I still feel drained. Every bit of me is tired, right down to my bones.

I clean my teeth and splash a bit of water on my face, and then I find a clean pair of pyjamas and climb into bed. As soon as my head hits the pillow I feel them, and it all comes back to me. I remember putting them carefully in a place where I knew they'd be safe because they, more than anything else, are too precious to risk any danger coming to them. I reach my hand under the pillow and feel the reassuring bulkiness of Mum's diaries, safe and sound and next to me. I think that maybe, I'm not as awful a person as I thought I was.

Six Months After: Today

The house is really quiet. I've found this the hardest thing to cope with since everything changed. It's not like we were the noisiest family in the world or anything, but when I walked in from school there would be talking and the noise of our house – washing machine whirring in the corner, back door slamming in the wind and threatening to break the glass, feet running up and down the stairs. I remember all the times I got mad because I couldn't find a quiet place to just *think*. I'd do anything now to be standing here in the hall with the sounds of life going on around me. Now I have too much time to think – I'm fed up with thinking.

So I've developed a sort of habit. First thing I do when I walk in the door at three thirty is shout 'hello' out of the back door. Dad can't hear me from the studio and I don't want to disturb him because he has to finish his work before Isaac returns, but it makes me feel I'm actually home. Next, I go into the living room and turn the TV on – not really loudly but just so I can hear it when I'm in the kitchen. After that, I put on the kettle (loudest kettle in the universe, Mum used to say) and go upstairs to Isaac's room. I never used to go inside his room voluntarily – all the stinky socks on the floor are enough to make your eyes water – but now I creep in and turn on his iPod. I make sure it's on shuffle and the volume on high.

When I've done all this, I go into my own room and get changed. I always have tons of homework so I take my books down to the kitchen. I've experimented to know exactly how loud I need the TV and Isaac's iPod – so that when I'm in the kitchen I can hear enough to make the house feel less empty, but not so much that I can't do my work.

Except I can't really concentrate on the maths problem in front of me, because something a little bit brilliant happened today. I wasn't expecting it – in fact I had to ask him to repeat himself cos I didn't actually think I'd heard him properly. It's been so long since I had a real conversation with anyone at school that I'm surprised I could even remember how to speak without sounding a total idiot. When Ben walked over to me I assumed he needed to find something out, like when our English project is due in. When he asked me how I was doing, I didn't really know what to say. I think I muttered some randomly stupid comment like 'very well, thank you', cos I suddenly felt shy and a bit embarrassed. Which is a new feeling for me right now – I haven't really felt anything for a while.

So when he said that he was going to the cinema at the weekend and did I want to go with him, I was a bit distracted and didn't hear him. He stood there for a moment, turning redder and redder, until I realized that I'd missed something and asked him to say it again. Of course, when I heard what he was saying I instantly managed to outdo him in the blushing stakes – I massively hate that feeling of boiling lava flooding across your face, knowing that you can't do a single thing to stop it. After all that drama with Alice, I didn't think that Ben even liked me any more – turns out I was wrong.

I wish I had someone to tell. This is the biggest event of the decade and I'm sitting here all on my own with only my stupid maths homework for company. I know that Alice would be pleased for me – I saw on Facebook that she's going out with Jack. Her new profile picture is of Jack giving her a piggyback. She's laughing like mad and waving at the camera. It looks like they're having a lot of fun. I know she'd have loved telling me about Jack for herself if I'd answered her messages, but it's never felt like the right time to call her. And what would I say? Much easier to keep hiding out in the library at lunchtimes and pretend that I haven't read her messages on Facebook. I like seeing what she's up to, though – I like seeing her happy. And actually, I secretly look forward to Friday nights when Alice sends me a long, chatty email about who's going out with who and what she's been doing all week. She wrote to me at the start and said she understood that I didn't want to talk about it. She said that she wouldn't mention it if that's what I wanted, but she was there for me when I was ready to hang out again. However long it took. I bet she never thought it'd take this long, though.

Anyway, it'd be great to have someone to talk to about today. I could tell Dad and Isaac, but Isaac won't really get it and Dad will just start freaking out about me going out with a boy. And he might even think he needs to have 'that conversation' with me, which would be excruciating for both of us.

No, I'll just have to keep this one to myself. It's probably not such a big deal anyway, although, for some reason that I'm not sure about, I feel a bit different. Everything you ever see about liking someone, or them liking you, shows hearts – big, beating hearts, lovesick hearts, broken hearts. My heart feels just like it did this morning – but my tummy feels weird. There's a tiny warm little ember, burning away in there, and it's making me feel a little less lonely and like maybe there's more to my day than doing homework.

I finally finish my maths problems and sit for a while at the kitchen table, thinking about Ben. I remember that day before the funeral when I saw him post an envelope through our front door. I didn't want to open it at the time and shoved it in the back of the drawer next to my bed. Now, though, I feel curious, and before I can change my mind I race upstairs and into my room. It only takes me a second to find it, a bit crumpled but otherwise fine.

I sit on my bed and carefully peel back the

envelope. We were sent about a million cards when it happened, all saying things like *In Deepest Sympathy* and *Sorry For Your Loss*. They were really depressing, those cards – not a single bright colour between them and most of them with pictures of lilies. Mum hated lilies. She said they were unnatural and fake and they smelt like misery. Not one person sent a picture of a daffodil or a primrose or a dandelion.

Ben hasn't sent me anything like those cards, though. I pull out a thick piece of folded paper and turn it over. There's a photograph stuck on the front and I can tell straight away that Ben made this himself. I look at the photo for a while, tracing my fingers over the faces. It was taken on the last day of term before Christmas, back when everything was good. I can't remember who took it but it wasn't Ben because he's in the picture, pulling a daft face, one of his arms thrown round Jack. Alice is in front of them, totally unaware that Jack is making bunny-ears behind her head. And I am there too. Right in the middle. I am looking at the camera and doing my best dramatic pose and I am laughing. We're all laughing.

I open up the card and read what Ben has written. He's a boy, so it's not exactly poetry. He's sorry. He doesn't know what to say. He's scared about making it worse. He thinks I must be really strong. He wants me to remember that I've got friends. He's sorry. I close it up and look again at the picture. It's perfect. Mum would have loved this card – if it were hers she'd have slipped it inside her diary and kept it forever, however long that might be.

I walk across the room to my pinboard. It used to be full of my favourite photographs but it's been bare for a while now. I pin Ben's card right in the middle and then head out to the hall. Isaac's got really bad taste in music, I think to myself, so I brave his room again and turn his iPod off, navigating carefully round his stinky, special box that today is slap-bang in front of his door. I look around his room and smile – it really is disgusting, but I guess it's how he wants it. As I turn to leave, I catch sight of the memory box that Dad gave him, poking out from under his bed. I know it's an invasion of his privacy, but he'll never know if I have a sneaky little peek inside.

I kneel down on the floor (having flicked his stinky socks away with my foot first) and pull out the box. I open the lid. The old sock and the teaspoon have gone, although the friendship bracelet and the bookmark are still there. Next to them is a picture that Isaac has drawn showing Mum, Dad, him and me. He's drawn little stick figures and labelled them with our names, and then drawn a great big circle round us all. We look a bit demented, with huge heads and tiny bodies, but we've all got crazily big smiles and we look safe, snuggled up together inside the circle. I pick up the drawing and see that underneath it is a Post-it note. I recognize the handwriting instantly and know that it's a note from Mum to Isaac – she used to put them in our lunchbox if she thought we might have a hard day.

I sit for a while, staring at the picture until my right leg goes to sleep and it starts to get cold. Dad will have taken Isaac to get our Friday night takeaway and they'll be back soon. We've had to make quite a few new rules around here since Mum died, but Isaac's coped really well, specially as some of our old rules have stayed the same. I suppose we're doing OK – Dad can work from home so he's around for Isaac and me, and Leah comes to see us as much as she can. I know they all miss Mum as much as I do, but they haven't stopped doing everything like I have. Sometimes I see Dad looking really sad but he'll see me watching and tell me he's just remembered something brilliant about Mum, and that it makes him feel happy and sad at the same time and actually, that's OK. I think what a relief it would be to find something funny, or allow myself to remember something good.

Before I can think too much about what I'm doing, I put Isaac's picture on the floor and go back downstairs. I stop in the hall and pick up the phone. I'm not sure what'll happen but I know that I'm tired of feeling lonely and unhappy. I think about what Mum said to me, that last day – that she knows I'm ready to live life loudly. I definitely haven't been doing *that* recently – more like creeping around as quietly as possible, trying not to attract any attention in case something else bad happens. Don't get me wrong. I'm not ready to party. But I am starting to realize that I won't forget Mum if I'm not busy being utterly miserable all the time.

Alice picks up the phone after the second ring. I tell her that I've missed her and ask if there's any chance we could meet up? She tells me that it's about time, she's been waiting for my phone call and we've got a lot of catching up to do, so best if I bring my toothbrush and sleeping bag to her house tomorrow. We chat for a bit and arrange to meet at our corner in the morning.

I put the phone down and take a deep breath. I feel lighter – Alice still likes me. I am a friend, I am part of something good. I walk back upstairs and into Isaac's room, keen to put his memory box away before he comes home. Kneeling down by his bed, I carefully pick up his family portrait and look at it one more time. It would feel pretty good to be smiling like I am on his crazy picture.

Just as I'm putting it back in, I see that there's something else, lying in the corner of the box. It's a bit squashed and it's really dried out – but there's no mistaking that it's a bald, naked dandelion head on a withered stem. Isaac put one of the dandelions from Mum's room into his memory box.

And suddenly, memories of that day and a thousand other days come flooding into my head. I try to resist them at first because I don't think I can handle any more pain, but then I realize that even though I'm crying, I don't feel quite so empty inside. I remember Mum, laughing her head off as she pointed at all the pots that we'd placed around her room. I remember how she cuddled me and how she smelt. I remember how much I love her and how, even when I was mad at her, she always let me know that she loved me and was proud of me.

And I think, kneeling there on Isaac's floor, that maybe it's going to be all right. I finally understand that Mum has gone and that, just like Isaac, I've got my own way of remembering her. I know that, even though we'll still have bad days, days when it's hard to remember how we ever used to be happy, that it's OK to think about Mum and to have fun and to laugh. I think that maybe, somewhere, Mum knows that Ben asked me out today and is cheering loudly (while telling me to be sensible, not wear too much make-up, charge my phone battery and definitely tell Dad where I'm going!).

I leave Isaac's room, head into my bedroom and take my own memory box out from the wardrobe. I put it on the bed, remove the lid and pick up the pile of diaries I've hidden carefully inside. I find the last diary, from 1989, and open it. I want to read the last thing that Mum wrote and I'm really hoping it's something amazing that I can remember forever. I skim through all the entries that I've already looked at and then stop. The rest of the diary is just a mass of blank pages with an occasional scribbled note, saying something really boring like *cinema at 7.30* or *choir practice*.

I start to flick through the pages, fighting the prickle of tears that I can feel behind my eyes. I wanted Mum's final words to be important, to mean something to me. As I get towards the back of the diary a piece of paper falls out on the floor. I kneel down and unfold it, and at first I can't figure out what it is. It's all crumpled and there are two different styles of handwriting – I recognize one as Mum's but I don't know who the other one belongs to. I start reading and realize it's a note, passed between Mum and her best friend, Beth, when they were fifteen.

12 February 1990
Destroy this note after reading!

Why are you in such a happy mood today? You've been grinning like a mad woman all lesson! Beth x

I don't know - life feels good I s'pose! Rachel xx

Not got anything to do with a certain boy, has it? You know — the one you're utterly besotted with! Beth x

Maybe! Just happy to be alive today, that's all! Over and out, Rachel xx

And that's it. *Happy to be alive. Over and out.* I fold the note and put it back inside the diary. Then I stand up and sit on my bed. No momentous final words here then. I am struggling to hold back my disappointment. I know it's probably stupid but I thought that Mum's last entry in her diary might help me out a bit.

For a moment I can feel myself sinking back into the place I've spent the last few months – but then I realize that I'm also imagining Mum, as a teenager, having fun with her best friend. I think about everything I've read in her diaries and realize that I can see her clearly in my head. I imagine her having a good day and not caring about what might happen in the future cos she was too busy thinking about boys and friends and having fun.

I've been feeling angry that she didn't write me a final letter – you know, the sort of thing you read about in books or see in films – something that I could keep with me and read at important times, like if I ever get married or have children. I thought she hadn't left any of her behind. But maybe that's why she gave me these diaries. Everything she's written in here is funny and honest and embarrassing and real – they *are* my mum.

I open up my memory box. Dad reprinted all the photos I had before that horrible day five months ago. Not much has changed since then except I go to school when I'm supposed to and Dad found someone for me to talk to each week about how I'm feeling. Sometimes I don't have anything to talk about, but apparently that's OK. I don't feel furious all of the time either – at least, I've stopped feeling angry with Mum. I know that she was really ill and I can't blame her for dying. I still can't help feeling that she didn't have to die, but I suppose that doesn't have to be anybody's fault. I've started taking a few photos again too. Nothing special, just things I see that make me feel – something.

I find the photo I took of me and Mum, the day she taught me about make-up and let me give her a makeover. I haven't put up a single photograph of Mum in my room – I just couldn't face the idea of seeing her every time I opened my eyes in the morning and knowing that she wasn't here any more. I've tried so hard to forget all the terribleness of Mum dying that I've let myself forget all the good stuff too. Mum has gone – but my memories of her will always be here.

I take the picture out of the box, smiling inside

at the awful faces we're pulling as we pose for the camera, and I stick it up on my pinboard, next to the card from Ben. Then I open up my jewellery box and take out the dangly earrings that Mum bought me the day I got my ears pierced. I could have worn them months ago, but it seemed wrong somehow. I carefully take out my studs and put the dangly earrings in. It takes me a few attempts but I get there in the end, and I'm grinning as I remember that fantastic day with Mum. I think about all the rules she tried to teach me and know that there's no chance of me forgetting her and that I need to let myself remember. I'll remember her every time I make spaghetti Bolognese, every time I put on make-up. I'll remember her when I'm laughing with my friends or shopping for underwear. She worked so hard to make sure that I could survive this time – right down to buying me clothes that I didn't need and that were too big, so I didn't have to rely on Dad to take me shopping. She taught me that I shouldn't forget how much I need my friends and made sure that we shared some important stuff – little things to anyone else, but huge to me. My mum had a plan and I can see now that I've not been following the rules. I know she didn't want to leave me and that she tried really hard to stay with us, but she just didn't have a choice.

Mum always said that the way to get started on something is to stop talking and start doing. So I turn round and head downstairs with my dangly earrings swishing against my ears, ready to start doing what Mum has always wanted me to do.

Live.

Acknowledgements

Many thanks to the people who read this book in its infancy and gave me massive support, particularly my fantastic mum and sister, Kerry and Elizabeth. Your belief in me leaves me lost for words.

Thank you to my fabulous friend Polly, for spending many hours reading through the early manuscript and offering your brilliant advice.

I am also hugely grateful to Shirley, Dan, Alison, Esther, Kedi, Kate and Niki – your thoughtful comments and feedback turned out to be exactly what I needed.

And thank you, Julia and Alex, for taking a chance and making this happen.

Violet Ink

REBECCA WESTCOTT

Coming in summer 2014

Turn over for an exclusive extract
from Rebecca's next book.

Mellow Yellow

I am a hundred per cent determined to win. Never, in living memory has Alex lost a game of Snap, but tonight history is about to be rewritten. In fact, it's my New Year's resolution. I have decided that this year is going to be the Year of Yellow and that means the Year of Happiness because yellow is a very happy colour. Winning this game against Alex is definitely going to make me happy. I crack my knuckles and wiggle my fingers – best to be flexible and ready for ninja-like moves.

'OK,' says Mum, shuffling the cards. Our deck is ancient, all dog-eared and crumpled. 'Are we all agreed on the rules?'

'Bring it on,' says Alex, sounding confident. I just nod, not taking my eyes off the cards that Mum is dealing out on to the kitchen table. When all the cards have been shared out between the three of us, we each pick up our pile, keeping the cards face down so that they can't be seen.

'Your turn to go first,' Mum says to me.

I put down the first card, turning it over as it reaches the table. Alex slams a card on top and the game has begun.

Jack, Two, Queen, Ace. I am totally focused, looking at nothing but the cards mounting up in front of me. My mouth is half open, the 's' ready on my lips. I WILL beat her this time – there's no way she can win again.

Three, Ten, Jack, King, King.

'Sn–' I start, but unbelievably my noisy, annoying big sister gets there before me.

'Cheese sandwiches!' she yells, nearly deafening me, and whacking her hand down on top of the stack of cards, just in case we're in any doubt about who has won. 'I win! Again!'

I cannot actually believe that this is happening. She's going to be utterly unbearable now. I really thought I'd win this time. I'd just like to win ONCE – is that too much to ask? I think I'd be a pretty good winner too and not do what Alex is doing now, making 'loser' signs at us and dancing round the kitchen bragging. I'd just smile generously and say, 'Good game.' Well, I think I would.

It's hard to know what I'd do when I never actually get to win. Ever.

Mum is laughing and Alex sinks back into her chair, looking across at me with a huge grin on her face.

'How, how –?' I splutter, but I can't even get the words out properly. 'It's not right, Alex. You've GOT to be cheating. We made you say "cheese sandwiches" – there was no way you could win.'

'What can I say?' says Alex, flicking her hair behind her shoulder and shrugging. I'm sure she'll think of something though; she's never usually short of a word or two. 'Natural talent, I guess. If there was an A level in playing Snap then I'd get an A star, that's for sure!'

'Well, it's totally unfair,' I tell her, feeling cross. 'We have to play again and this time you've got to say "cheese and mayonnaise sandwiches". And NO cheating.'

I grab the cards and start to reshuffle the deck, but Mum stops me.

'Not tonight, Izzy. Alex has got studying to do and, sadly for her, Snap is not one of her A level subjects, so she needs to put a bit of effort into doing some work.'

Alex groans dramatically. Alex does everything dramatically actually, like her entire life is really a show and she's the star. It means that she's noisy and bossy and very opinionated, but it also makes her a pretty exciting person to live with. You never quite know what she's going to do next – the only thing you do know is that it won't be boring. In the whole seventeen years that Alex has been alive I don't think she's ever done anything average. Not like me. My name could be the definition of average.

'Do you *have* to remind me? We haven't even gone back to school yet. I was just starting to relax.' She scowls at Mum. 'It's very important that I have rest sessions in between all the hard work you know – all my teachers say so. Stress can be very damaging at this stage of my life.'

Mum stands up and starts to clear away our leftover dinner plates. 'Stress can be very damaging at my time of life too, I'll have you know. And I think you'll find the most important part of what you just said was the bit about resting in between working. WORKING! And, as I've seen precious little evidence of you doing any actual work over the Christmas holidays, I think you'll survive with a shorter "relaxation" session tonight!'

She is smiling at Alex, but in that way that means 'do what I say or I'll stop pretending that you have a choice'. Alex pushes back her chair and gets up, pulling a face when Mum has turned towards the sink.

'Sorry, Izzy. I'll have to thrash you at Snap another night.'

'No rush,' I mutter. 'I'm probably going to be really busy with violin practice for the next few weeks.'

'Oh joy. More screeching and wailing to set my teeth on edge.' Alex grimaces at me as she leaves the room, her pile of school books still on the table and her jumper and scarf hanging over the back of her chair. She'll be back down in ten minutes, once she's spent a while making her room right for studying. That doesn't mean that she'll tidy it up. No. Alex says that the ambience has to be right so she'll drape a silk scarf over her lamp and light some joss sticks, and then flit around lighting candles all over the place.

It drives Mum crazy – she's terrified that Alex is going to burn the house down – but Alex says it's her room and she's virtually an adult so Mum should trust her for a change. Mum lets her, but what Alex doesn't know is that, when she's asleep,

Mum always creeps into her bedroom and checks everything is safe. I know this because I check on her too, and one night I opened my bedroom door just as Mum was going into Alex's room. I saw her tiptoe round the room, turning off the lamp and making sure that the candles were out. When she came out, I pretended that I was going to the bathroom. Mum gave me a hug and put her finger to her lips and I knew that she didn't want Alex to know that Mum still looks after her.

I'm glad that Alex has got me AND Mum to keep her safe because sometimes her head is so busy with exciting things, she forgets to do the things that she really should be doing. We're like her protectors so that she can get on with being Alex.

Dandelion Clocks

Reading Group Questions

1. *Dandelion Clocks* is written in the first person, from the point of view of Liv. Do you think the story would have had less/more impact if it had been written in the third person?

2. Which character would you most like to meet? What would you ask them?

3. How would you describe the relationship between Isaac and Liv? Do you think they both rely on each other equally or does one need the other more?

4. Mum tells Liv that she's ready to live life loudly. What do you think Mum means when she says this?

5. How do Liv's feelings towards her mum change at the start/middle/end of the book?

6. Who do you think is the bravest character in the book? Who has the most courage?

7. Despite the sadness of the story, there are some funny moments in *Dandelion Clocks*. Are there any scenes that you identify with and think 'that could have happened to me'?

8. Isaac has Asperger's syndrome and finds it difficult to understand idioms (phrases that mean something different to what is actually said). So when Liv tells him to 'speak to the hand' he literally talks to his hand. How many idioms can you think of that are used in everyday language? For example: *It's raining cats and dogs* = raining heavily, or *spill the beans* = tell a secret.

9. How is the theme of *rules* used throughout *Dandelion Clocks*?

10. Liv says, 'I'm kind of obsessed with photographs. I love the way that they're memory evidence.' What does she mean by this?

11. Liv is a character who often leaps to the wrong conclusion. How does this get her into trouble on several occasions?

12. How does the mood of the book change after Mum has died? How does Liv change?

13. Did you like the ending? How would you have liked it to end?

14. At the end of the book, Liv decides that she needs to remember her mum's rules and try to live life loudly. What do you think happens to Liv after the book ends?

Writing Activity

Do you keep a diary? I've been writing diaries since I was eight years old and most of the entries are either really boring or completely embarrassing! I used some of my own diary entries as Mum's diary in *Dandelion Clocks*. For example, I really did have a guinea pig called Smokey and I cried every night for weeks when he died. I also had a list of four and a half boys that I really liked, but I was definitely not in the cool group at school and all the boys thought that I was loud and annoying.

When I was eighteen, I spent hours writing meaningful song lyrics in the margins with felt-tip pens (I said I was uncool . . .). I really like reading my old diaries and remembering how I felt when I was a child and then a teenager, even if they do make me cringe.

Writing a diary from the point of view of someone else can really improve your writing. It's important to write events in a chronological order and to make the tone of your writing really personal. Using rhetorical questions (a question that won't be answered) can help the reader understand how the writer is feeling and give us more information about their state of mind.

Try writing a diary entry for each of these characters – and maybe start keeping your own diary. You don't need to use anything special – you can write in an old notebook. Fill in your own *Secret File* page to help you get started!

1. A well-known celebrity who has had a bad day and discovers that they are splashed across the front pages of the newspapers.
2. A character from a children's picture book. I'd love to read the diary of the Hungry Caterpillar, hearing about his week from his point of view!
3. Your own diary entry from the day you made your biggest mistake. Include one lie – something that didn't really happen.
4. Liv's diary entry from the day she goes on her date with Ben. What happens? Does it go well? How does she feel when she gets home?

Questions for Rebecca

How long did it take you to write *Dandelion Clocks* and *Violet Ink*?
I tend to write a first draft quite quickly – it takes me about six to eight weeks, writing after work in the evenings and at weekends. Being a teacher is great because I get lots of writing time during the holidays, which helps! Once the first draft is written I'll take my time on the edit, really developing the voice of the main character and making sure that there are no inconsistencies in the plot.

Does anyone read your books while you are in the process of writing them?
I'm really lucky to have an incredibly supportive family, who read everything that I write (and have an opinion on everything I write too!). My eleven-year-old daughter was the first person to read both books. In fact, it was a conversation that I had with her in

our garden one day last spring that gave me the idea for *Dandelion Clocks*. She also helped me to write some of Izzy's poems in *Violet Ink*. Once I'm happy with what I've written, I'll ask people to have a read and give me their thoughts. My husband, mum, sister and lovely friends are great at doing this!

Which authors have inspired you?
One of my favourite authors is Robert Cormier. He writes about topics that are quite grown up in a way that younger readers can access, without being patronizing. I often find his books chilling – they always leave me with a list of questions and wanting more.

When I was a child, I loved Judy Blume. I would read her books and feel as if I completely knew the characters, even though their lives were so different to mine.

Now, I enjoy reading books by authors like Patrick Ness, Meg Rosoff and John Green. They aren't afraid of tackling 'big' issues. After all, life happens to everyone – not just to adults.

What is your favourite way to spend a day off from teaching and writing?
I love spending time with my family. We are all big fans of camping and what I enjoy most is sitting in the sunshine watching my husband cook us an amazing campfire meal while our three children race around

on their bikes (I'm not completely lazy though – I do the washing-up!).

In the winter, if I'm not writing then I'm probably reading, while my husband cooks us a meal and the children create chaos with Nerf guns. (You can probably tell that I really, really hate cooking.) Actually, I'm not that fond of housework either, so at the weekends we play a card game after supper – the loser has to do the washing up.

I want to be a writer. What are your top tips for getting published?

Write for fun! When I wrote *Dandelion Clocks* I was so excited by the idea that I wanted to write it down just to find out if I could create a story from beginning to end. I didn't write to get published – I wrote because it made me feel happy.

Sometimes, write as quickly as you possibly can. Don't worry about whether it's perfect – just enjoy the excitement of writing your words down. And then leave it. One of my favourite things about writing is returning to read something I wrote a while ago. It's a great way of figuring out what works in your writing.

Write for lots of different reasons. Being a writer doesn't mean that you are writing a book. It means that you communicate and record information using written words. So write a diary, write letters, write emails, send texts. Make lists, write a poem that you'll only ever show one person, leave notes for your family on the fridge in magnetic letters. Write using as many exciting, interesting words as you can and then write using only twenty words. Play about – they're your words and there aren't any rules.

Don't give up. If someone gives you feedback on your writing (it could be your friends, family or a teacher), then listen to what they have to say. Try out their ideas and decide if it improves your writing. If it does, then great – you've developed your skills. If it doesn't, then you haven't lost anything.

Rebecca's Top 5

Best books

Goodnight Mister Tom by Michelle Magorian
After the First Death by Robert Cormier
Wonder by R. J. Palacio
A Monster Calls by Patrick Ness
Skallagrigg by William Horwood
(But really, it's impossible to choose just five! I have always loved The Dark Is Rising trilogy by Susan Cooper and I've recently started reading books by John Green. When I was growing up my reading included Enid Blyton, Judy Blume, Willard Price, Lynne Reid Banks and Lucy M. Boston to name just a few. I've just read *Grace* by Morris Gleitzman and thought it was amazing.)

Favourite photos

Holidaying on the Isles of Scilly, we stumbled across a deserted beach with hundreds of Makka Pakka rocks. We stayed there for hours, adding our own contribution.

Me, aged five. Check out the dodgy haircut!

On holiday last year in France — I was terrified that the rope swing would break but I made myself swing across the river!

This photo makes me laugh! My family are very outdoorsy. I am less outdoorsy. We were in the French Alps and I look utterly lost, trying to find signal for my phone.

My little sister and me, aged six and fourteen. I am cuddling Bracken, the guinea pig I had when I (eventually!) recovered from the tragic death of Smokey.

Perfecting the art of pancake tossing, aged eleven.

I took this at a local festival. It was really muddy and my children went inside this storytelling shed. I like the way that the filthy wellies look as if they're waiting for feet to be returned to them.

Favourite foods
Pizza with extra pepperoni
Toast with crunchy peanut butter
Satsumas
Very spicy beef chilli with lots of fresh green chilli peppers
Butterscotch Angel Delight – it HAS to be butterscotch. Every other flavour is disgusting but this one tastes like a little bit of perfection!

Cosiest places to read
In bed, with a cup of tea
In the bath – I *hardly* ever drop my book in the water
Halfway up the stairs, looking through the window into the garden
In a tent, with the rain lashing down outside
Snuggled up next to a roaring fire (although I am a total fire-killer, and if I'm in charge then the fire will be less roaring and more spluttering)

Things to put in Room 101
Umbrellas: I have always disliked umbrellas. Sure, I get that they keep you dry but at what cost? If you're holding an umbrella, then you suddenly can't do anything that requires two hands and the risk of poking someone in the eye is dramatically increased. I would rather get wet or put my hood up (even if this does make me look a bit daft).

Cooking: I love eating but I really cannot stand cooking. When I was younger I used to believe that it was something I'd grow to enjoy – but one husband and three kids later I can honestly say that I loathe cooking. And making packed lunches. My repertoire is basically limited to chilli, spaghetti Bolognese, pesto pasta and baked potatoes. Perhaps it isn't surprising that I married an excellent cook and our children are fast becoming great chefs . . .

Self-service checkouts at supermarkets: These send me into a crazy, ranting rage every time I use them. Unexpected item in baggage area? I don't think there is, *actually*. I always seem to do something wrong and then have to spend so long apologizing to the poor checkout assistant that it would have been quicker to just queue up for a normal till in the first place.

Dog poo: Nobody would say that they actively LIKE poo, but I routinely ruin walks with my family by alerting them to the presence of every single bit of poo that we encounter along the way. I can't help it – I just don't trust them not to step in it and then the rest of my day will be spent cleaning their trainers. Getting rid of dog poo would make me very happy (I'm not that bothered about other kinds of poo).

Excessive use of exclamation marks: Just kidding! If I am Queen of anything then it's Queen of Exclamation Marks. I love them and firmly believe that you can never have too many. My great-granny used to say of chocolates that 'one's a tease'. I think the same can be said of exclamation marks!!!!!!!

Liv's Playlist

1. 'Lovely Day' by Bill Withers (A bit of an oldie but brilliant. My dad puts this on when he's in a good mood and sometimes I'd see him and mum dancing together in the kitchen. I played this all night after Ben smiled at me. Some days are totally perfect!)

2. 'Prince Charming' by Adam & The Ants (I looked up this band on YouTube after I read the diary entry where Mum wrote that they were her favourite. They're OK, I s'pose. The video's pretty funny!)

3. Pokemon theme tune (Not on MY playlist but I'm forced to listen to it for hours on end when Isaac decides it's his tune of the day.)

4. 'Welcome Home' by Radical Face (this was on my iPod when Dad brought Mum back from St Mary's Hospice. I really, truly love this song.)

5. 'This Little Light Of Mine' (We sang this song at Mum's funeral. I can't listen to it without crying, but I know that Mum is somewhere, watching over me and telling me to let my light shine.)

6. Brahms' Lullaby (I asked Dad what the lullaby was that I sang to Mum the last time I saw her. He didn't know but I sang it to Leah and she told me it was Brahms' Lullaby and she downloaded it for me from iTunes. Sometimes I go to sleep with my earphones in and this on my iPod and I imagine that Mum is singing me to sleep.)

7. 'Here comes the Sun' by The Beatles (This was one of Mum's favourite songs. Playing this song makes me think about Mum doing the washing up and singing at the top of her voice. It makes me smile.)

8. 'Hall of Fame' by The Script (I listen to this when I want to remind myself of what Mum wanted me to do – to LIVE LIFE LOUDLY and be the best that I can be.)

Sources of advice

If you or someone you know has been bereaved, you might find these websites helpful:
www.griefencounter.org.uk
www.winstonswish.org.uk

You might also find these fiction books helpful:

5+

Badger's Parting Gifts by Susan Varley
Michael Rosen's Sad Book by Michael Rosen and Quentin Blake

8+

Two Weeks with the Queen by Morris Gleitzman
The Cat Mummy by Jacqueline Wilson

10+

Cherry Crush by Cathy Cassidy

12+

The Fault in Our Stars by John Green
My Sister Jodie by Jacqueline Wilson
Vicky Angel by Jacqueline Wilson
A Monster Calls by Patrick Ness
My Sister Lives on the Mantelpiece by Annabel Pitcher